I0552541

OPERATION KILL IKE

Destroyers WWII Series
Book Five

Charles Whiting

SAPERE
BOOKS

OPERATION
KILL IKE

Published by Sapere Books.

24 Trafalgar Road, Ilkley, LS29 8HH

saperebooks.com

Copyright © Charles Whiting, 1975

Charles Whiting has asserted his right to be identified as the author of this work.
All rights reserved.

No part of this publication may be reproduced, stored in any retrieval system, or transmitted, in any form, or by any means, electronic, mechanical, photocopying, recording, or otherwise, without the prior written permission of the publishers.
This book is a work of fiction. Names, characters, businesses, organisations, places and events, other than those clearly in the public domain, are either the product of the author's imagination, or are used fictitiously.
Any resemblances to actual persons, living or dead, events or locales are purely coincidental.

ISBN: 978-1-80055-851-9

'As soon as we've won this war, Butch, I want to know everything about this German plan to kill me!'
The Supreme Commander in Europe, General Eisenhower to Lt-Commander Butcher USN, 27 December 1944

ONE: THE TREFF

'Our analysis of the contents of that bottle could well decide
the future course of the war — tell your destroyers that,
Lieutenant Crooke.'

Major Abel to Lt Crooke, CO of the Destroyers, 15 December 1944

CHAPTER 1

'War over by Christmas — official!' the old cloth-capped newspaperman at the corner yelled, his red nose dripping in the biting cold, as he thrust a copy of the *Daily Express* at the two officers in the back of the Humber staff car. Commander Miles Mallory, the assistant to the Head of Naval Intelligence, nestled deeper into his overcoat and shook his head.

'It's a nice thought anyway,' he said wearily, lighting another of his gold-ringed Morland Specials. One-eyed Lieutenant Crooke, VC, the CO of Naval Intelligence's special commando squad, the Destroyers, grunted and stared moodily out of the car window. In front of them their Wren driver waited patiently for the elderly special constable to allow them to move on.

To Crooke the London crowd looked especially grey and war-weary this cold December day. Outside the butcher's shop, bearing the legend 'Offal today — ration books A–H', the housewives, their hair stiff with iron curlers under their headscarves, gossiped listlessly in the long queue. A couple of ATS, their khaki stockings wrinkled at the knee, stood before a wall which bore the faded chalk scrawl, 'Second Front Now — 1942!' Their faces were pale and strained and there were dark shadows under their eyes. They stared blankly at the traffic piling up at the crossroads. Crooke wondered if the nation could stand another year of war. Five years were enough.

The constable had just given the signal to move on when the air-raid sirens started their stomach-turning howl. Hurriedly he waved the cars into the kerb. The Wren pulled the Humber over as the constable panted across to them, pulling on his white helmet. He saluted when he saw the two officers.

'Handbrake on, please! Windows open on account of the blast — and into that doorway yonder!'

'Must we, Constable?' Mallory asked, stubbing out his cigarette irritably. 'We've an urgent appointment.'

''Fraid so, sir. Them doodlebugs is real buggers — if you'll pardon my French!'

The three of them crouched in the nearest doorway while all along the street other people did the same. In a few moments the noise of the traffic had stopped. Along the whole length of the Strand they waited for the now familiar chug-chug of Hitler's new weapon — the flying bomb.

They did not have long to wait. From the east came the faint but unmistakable sound of a doodlebug.

'Sounds like the old two-stroke motorbike I used to have at Eton,' Mallory said.

Crooke tugged at his black eyepatch and searched the sky for the attackers. 'There it is!' he shouted suddenly.

At St James's Park the 3.7-inch anti-aircraft guns opened up with an angry roar. The Wren jumped. Mallory put out his hand to calm her. The Strand reverberated and echoed with their thunder. Red and yellow balls of flame exploded in the sky, disappearing in bursts of grey smoke. But the vengeance weapons, with which Hitler hoped to break London's spirit, still came on.

Suddenly the flak stopped. From the west one of the new, clipped-wing Spitfires came zooming in at a tremendous speed. Flashing through the balls of smoke, it came level with the first flying bomb. A distance of perhaps fifty feet separated the two aircraft now.

'My God,' said Mallory, 'that pilot's got some nerve.'

'He's going to try to tip its wing,' Crooke said. 'Deflect it away from the city.'

The two aircraft came closer and closer until the Spitfire pilot turned in on the flying bomb with a half roll and his wing nudged the doodlebug. The flying bomb's engine cut out abruptly and its black nose tipped downwards. There was a tremendous explosion. A great wind roared down the Strand. A building collapsed, the windscreen of the Humber shattered. Glass cascaded all around them. The Wren screamed. There were yells of pain. Then the blast proper enveloped them. The Humber was lifted up as if by a gigantic hand and dumped on its side. Most of its roof had been blown off. Flames were already beginning to lick greedily at its paintwork.

Mallory let go of the Wren. 'My briefcase!' he yelled.

'*Get back!*' Crooke cried. '*It'll go up at any moment.*' With a dull boom the petrol tank exploded. A cloud of oily black smoke shot into the air. Flames crackled all around the wreck. Far off ambulance bells started to ring.

Mallory raised the Wren gently from her knees, to which she had sunk in shock. 'It's all right now,' he said gently. 'They're gone.'

The Wren opened her eyes and screamed again. '*Look!*' They followed the direction of her gaze. A head lay in the centre of the debris-littered Strand. A few feet away the body of its owner was sprawled out. It was the newspaperman. The *Daily Express* poster was still tied around the headless torso's waist, mocking it with the announcement: 'WAR OVER BY CHRISTMAS — OFFICIAL!'

CHAPTER 2

White's Club was busy. Now the air-raid sirens had sounded the all clear, the civilians from the ministries and the red-tabbed senior officers were emerging from the Club's shelters and heading for the bar for a quick drink before they returned to their offices.

Pushing his way after Mallory, Crooke listened to their conversation with mounting distaste. The same complacent crowd, full of their own importance, he thought to himself, quite unaware that the British Empire was falling to pieces all around them. Now they were getting ready to take over again, convinced that the war was all over bar the shouting.

'There he is,' Mallory said. 'Next to that chap in the fancy suit.' Crooke dismissed his contemptuous thoughts as he looked along the bar to the other end where the man who had summoned them so urgently that morning was sitting. He was a skinny, pale-faced man with thinning hair, dressed in a dark suit, the only splash of colour his Old Etonian tie. He looked ill. Surprisingly enough, however, in spite of the press of important people pushing into the bar, he and his companion had plenty of room. No one seemed prepared to infringe on their privacy and Crooke knew why. The man at the end of the bar was one of the most powerful men in London; he was 'C', the head of the British Secret Intelligence Service.

At last he put down his glass of sherry and indicated that they should come across.

'Good of you to come, Mallory,' he said. He nodded to Crooke frostily. 'Hello.' There was a thin smile on his narrow lips, but no warmth in his eyes.

He turned to his companion. 'Peter,' he said, 'be a good chap and leave us now. Tell Vivian I'll be back in the office in about an hour.'

'Yes sir.' His assistant finished his drink and disappeared. 'C' did not offer to buy the two newcomers a drink but got down to business at once, as if their presence were a little distasteful to him and he wanted to be finished with them as soon as possible.

'Now then, Mallory,' he began, 'we're in a bit of a fix. Most of my chaps are out in the field with this Operation Flashpoint. You've heard of it no doubt?'

'You mean the op to saturate the Rhineland with turncoat Germans who will guide our forward troops into position when the January offensive starts?'

'That's right. Lot of German POWs involved. As the PM says, the German is either at your throat or grovelling at your feet. Now we're winning, they're prepared to risk their necks to work for us. Anyway that's where most of my boys are.'

Listening in silence, Crooke was again amazed at the way 'C' discussed top-secret missions at the bar of the club. Some of the more critical of the wartime recruits to the Secret Intelligence Service said that the real headquarters of the SIS was in this bar and not in the official building in the Broadway. But still, he supposed that 'C' thought the men around him would never betray any secret they chanced to overhear; after all, most of them had been to the same school and served in the Brigade.

'It's Eisenhower's idea and he got the PM to overrule me on this one.'

'Overrule you?'

'Yes, I wanted my chaps to have a closer look at the situation in the Rhineland rather than get bogged down on this op. To my way of thinking there are several factors which indicate that the Germans are not yet ready to throw in the sponge. Look at the way they're defending the Rhineland at the moment. The Americans took 5,000 casualties in the Huertgen Forest alone last week. Nearly a division of riflemen. Then these V-weapons.' He hesitated a moment and licked his lips. 'What if the Germans have something worse up their sleeve — something even more terrifying than the rockets? That's why I've asked Rushbrooke to let me have you, and those chaps of yours.' 'C' looked vaguely at Crooke, as if seeing him for the first time. Almost conversationally, he said, 'I'm sure you're well aware, Crooke, that I like neither you nor your men.'

Crooke, who had won the VC and lost an eye during the 1942 attempt to murder Field-Marshal Rommel in the Western Desert, flushed hotly. Ever since he had struck the Deputy Commander, Home Forces on the nose because the latter had refused to allow him to return to active service after his convalescence, he knew he had been anathema to the military establishment, which included 'C'. He bit his lip and held his tongue.

'I have no time for the scum of the British Army,' 'C' continued. 'A unit which is composed of hired killers like yours. And I wouldn't use them if my own people were available, but they aren't, so I have no alternative but to use your Destroyers.' He shrugged his shoulders. 'Still, you've proved useful in the past and I hope you'll do the same now.'

He finished off the rest of his sherry. 'Now this is what I want you to do. I've cleared it with Admiral Rushbrooke,' he added, turning to the Commander again, who was eyeing the whisky bottle behind the bar. 'I want you and Crooke here to fly out with your team to Paris — to SHAEF Headquarters. There you'll be contacted by the representative of Project X.'

'His name?' Mallory interrupted.

'I don't know. The Project is very hush-hush for reasons you'll discover in Versailles. At all events their representative will brief you on your mission which, I may tell you, has top priority at the moment.'

'He won't,' Crooke said quietly.

'Oh, and why won't he, may I ask?' said 'C', just as softly.

'Because my hired killers, as you call them, are back where I found them in Egypt in 1942.'

'And where is that, pray?'

'A place where I am sure you'll agree they belong — in the glasshouse — to be exact, in Catterick Military Prison.'

CHAPTER 3

'*All right, you pregnant ducks, let's be having you! Outside on parade!*'
The hard voices of the NCOs shattered the morning stillness.
'*At the double now — outside!*'

Smartly the NCOs in their polished boots crunched down
the frozen gravel paths between the dreary wooden huts which
made up Catterick Military Prison, their breath fogging the air,
their cheeks gleaming a healthy red. Cracking their bamboo
swagger sticks against the doors and windows, they yelled
threateningly, '*Come on now — last man out's on a fizzer!*'

Inside the wooden huts the prisoners came to sudden and
violent life. It didn't pay to be late on parade at Number 54
Military Prison. The 'staffs' were only too eager to take the law
into their own hands — four or five of them at a time with
pick handles!

They gave their uniforms and equipment a last anxious
check. Hands ran down flies. Pockets were flapped — left,
right, hip, front. Thighs were tapped to check that the bulky
yellow field dressings were there. Little fingers were bored into
the muzzles of rifles to remove any last specks of dirt.
Cardboard-squared ammunition pouches were screwed round
to a more comfortable angle, gaiters tugged, toecaps rubbed on
the backs of immaculately creased trousers — soaped the night
before and placed under the mattress to be slept on.

Clumsily they clattered down the gravel paths into the grey
December morning, with the NCOs, hands on hips, barking
and shouting at them from all sides like so many sheepdogs:
'*Get fell in … horrible men … that stupid soldier there … like spare
dildoes in a convent… GET FELL IN!*' Hurriedly, their flushed

shining faces wreathed in the grey fog of their own breath, they formed up between the huts. Slowly, suspiciously the 'staffs' walked down the lines, checking each rigid soldier with hard-eyed thoroughness, ever aware that if they slipped up they might lose their stripes and be sent to the front. At last they were satisfied. Down the long lines of prisoners came the same series of commands, repeated anew by each platoon commander, 'Close order — close order, *march*! Cover off now!... Come on — smartish, bags of swank!'

Grateful for the chance to move their stiffened limbs, happy they had passed the first inspection of the day, the prisoners shuffled their feet rapidly until — somehow or other — they were in a straight line again.

'Stand at ease! Stand easy!'

They relaxed. An outbreak of coughing, the clanking of rifle-butts on the frozen concrete and then silence — for a moment.

'*Staff!*' a tremendous hysterical voice screamed from far away. '*That man in the second rank needs an haircut! Like a bleeding concert violinist!* Orderly sergeant — *take his name and last three numbers!*'

The prisoners stiffened with fear. The voice belonged to the RSM — Black Jack Coogan.

Black Jack stalked up the road, pacing stick under his arm, his sharp chin, with its black beard that no amount of talcum powder could hide, thrust forward aggressively, as if only too eager to look for trouble. As he came level with the waiting prisoners he slowed down and then, appearing to jump in the air, brought down his boots with a crash of hobnails against concrete. For a moment he said nothing, his dark, little eyes searching their rigid ranks for what he called 'low idle filthy men'. Then he spoke, the phrases coming out in short harsh barks.

'You men are going on parade in five minutes … big noise from the Admiralty … spot-on turnout… Woe betide any of you idle men if you bugger up…'

In the front rank of the nearest platoon someone broke wind, long, loud and insolently.

Black Jack's head shot round. 'Who was that low filthy man who did that?' he bellowed. 'Come on, out with it!' He glared at the men in fury, but there was no answer to his question. Angrily he stalked over to the front rank. 'Did you buggers not hear what I said?'

Silence. He thrust his jaw into the bronzed face of the little man nearest to him. 'Was it you, Stevens?' he snarled. The little Cockney Destroyer stared woodenly ahead.

'Me, Sarnt-Major?' he said out of the corner of his mouth. 'Not me, sir.'

Black Jack looked along the line of the Destroyers — Stevens, Yank, Peters, Thaelmann and Muhammed — suspiciously.

'I've got my eye on you lot,' he said, his voice suddenly soft and full of menace. 'You're a lot of bolshies, you are. A bunch of smart alecks, who think they're tough.' He poked the big pacing stick at them. 'But I've broken tougher buggers than you. You've got fifty-six days in here, remember, and I'm gonna make them fifty-six days of hell…'

'Sarnt-Major,' the orderly sergeant's voice broke into his tirade. He spun round.

'What is it?'

'The Adjutant's signalling, sir. Look's as if them Navy blokes is here.'

Black Jack stepped back smartly.

'All right then — watch it.' Swiftly he rapped out a series of orders. The prisoners stamped round to their right. To the sergeant-major's bellow of 'Swing them arms now! Let's have bags of swank', they started to march towards the square. As he passed Black Jack, Stevens broke wind again — long, loud and insolently.

Commander Mallory, dressed in Rear Admiral Rushbrooke's overcoat and gold-encrusted cap, followed by the Wren driver, clad in the uniform 'borrowed' from her section officer and Crooke, who was wearing Mallory's own expensive navy warm, walked slowly along the ranks of the prisoners. At his side the Commandant marched officiously, obviously pleased that his remote military prison had been honoured by a visit from the head of Naval Intelligence himself.

Mallory, Crooke thought, played his role of a bored but keen-eyed senior officer well. A couple of times he paused and, indicating a wooden-faced soldier staring rigidly into the distance, asked innocently, 'I say, Commandant, should that chap have his blouse button undone like that?'

Once Mallory paused in front of an old soldier, with the faded white and sand-coloured ribbon of the Africa Star on his chest and two wound stripes on his sleeve, and shook his head in mock sadness. He turned to the Commandant and speaking as if the man were not present, in the typical manner of a senior officer, he said, 'It's indicative of the way things are going when experienced soldiers like this chap end up in here.'

'Twenty-eight days, Admiral,' the Commandant explained. 'Absent without leave. His wife went off with a Pole.'

Mallory sniffed and passed on. Finally he stopped in front of the third platoon. Indicating the Destroyers, he asked innocently, 'And what are these rogues in for, Commandant?'

'Brawl with some American paratroopers, sir,' he answered. 'The one with the black eye' — he pointed to the oldest

18

member of the Destroyers — 'he started it, although he's a Yank himself apparently. At all events the five of them took on twelve Americans on leave from the 101st Airborne. Seven of the Yankees ended up in hospital, one with a serious concussion. These chaps landed up in here — with fifty-six days apiece.'

Mallory tut-tutted while the Destroyers stared ahead unwinkingly, as if their boss were a complete stranger to them. Then the little party passed on. Suddenly Mallory stopped before a young man at the end of the line. 'I say, Commandant,' he said in apparent outrage. 'Just look at the chap's boots.'

The Major peered down at the young man's boots. The products of hours of work with toothbrush, polish and a great deal of spit, they gleamed like mirrors.

'I can't see anything, sir,' he began hesitantly.

'The laces, *the laces*, man!' Mallory cut him short, angrily. The Commandant flushed in alarm.

'Sarnt-Major,' he snapped. 'Look at that man's laces.'

Black Jack, followed by the orderly sergeant, hurried forward. He stuck his pacing stick between the terrified young soldier's legs.

'Get them bloody legs apart!' he bellowed. 'Come on, you evil man!'

At the tail end of the procession, Crooke took quick advantage of the incident. The prisoners remained staring rigidly ahead, eyes directed on some unseen object in the far distance as Crooke thrust a small round container into Stevens' hand. The Cockney grasped it at once. His face turned to one side so that the men in the rear ranks could not see the movement of his mouth, Crooke hissed urgently, 'Give us five minutes to get off the parade ground. Drop it and run like hell.

We've got a car waiting outside the gate. *Understand?* Stevens' face did not change its wooden expression, but he winked. He'd understood.

The blue staff car had just swung past the 'staffs' guarding the gate of the Military Prison when Stevens dropped the tear-gas capsule. There was a soft plop and soon thick grey gas started to rise.

'Come on,' he yelled and dropped his rifle with a clatter on the concrete.

The other Destroyers needed no urging. They had recognised the top-secret SOE tear-gas capsule as soon as Stevens had dropped it. Letting their rifles fall as one and grasping the ends of their noses tightly, they broke ranks.

The choking gas spread swiftly and in seconds everything was in chaos and confusion around them. Tears streamed down the faces of the prisoners as they coughed and choked. The orderly sergeant tried to intercept the Destroyers but the Yank kneed him smartly.

'What the bloody hell's going on here?' Black Jack roared hysterically as they broke out of the cloud of thick smoke. Thaelmann, the German member of the Destroyers, punched him hard in the stomach. As he bent double with pain, Muhammed, the Egyptian, wrenched the pacing stick from his hands and stuck it into his rear viciously.

'Now yer know what yer can do with yer sodding Christmas pudden, sarnt major!' Stevens yelled as the RSM screamed with pain and shot forward full length on the parade ground. Moments later they were clambering the high wall, while the two 'staffs' at the gate fumbled with their .38s indecisively. One by one they dropped onto the frozen ground outside. The blue staff car was waiting for them, with Mallory at the wheel. Crooke flung open the back door.

'Come on,' he yelled. 'Let's get out of here before they court-martial the lot of us!'

Two hours later they were aboard an RAF Anson flying across the Channel, heading for Paris and SHAEF Headquarters. The mission had begun.

CHAPTER 4

They landed at one of the two workable runways in Orly Field just as the short December afternoon was beginning to draw to a close. The American Air Transport Command people housed in one of the temporary wooden barracks, which four months before had still been occupied by the German *Luftwaffe*, organized them an ancient Citroen taxi and they set off immediately for SHAEF at Versailles. But when they reached the huge combined headquarters they were doomed to disappointment. No one seemed to have heard of Project X. The officers of the hush-hush American organization, OSS, were polite but firm. Whatever Project X might be, they had no knowledge of it. British Military Intelligence had not heard of the organization either. In the end Mallory went right to the top, to Brigadier Ken Strong, Eisenhower's Chief-of-Intelligence.

The Intelligence Officer was polite but apparently as puzzled about their mission as everyone else at the Supreme Commander's HQ.

'I suggest,' he said finally, 'that you go back to Paris and check with your own people there!'

'You mean the SIS, Brigadier?'

'Yes. They've got an office in the capital again.' He mentioned the address. 'And the best of luck to you.'

Outside it was dark. The taxi driver grumbled, but allowed himself to be bribed with Mallory's last carton of Morland cigarettes — they would bring a small fortune on the Paris black market.

It was a long wearisome drive, with the Frenchman fighting the tail-to-tail trucks of the celebrated Red Ball supply column, which roared from the Channel ports right through France up to the front, twenty-four hours a day, seven days a week.

As they crawled along the blacked-out country roads, Crooke stared at his men, their faces illuminated every now and again by the headlights of the big trucks, the only vehicles in the combat zone to be allowed to drive with full lights. Their features still bore the traces of the brawl with the American paratroopers which had started over the usual drunken pub trivialities.

'Say, when are you limeys gonna get off your butts and do some goddamn fighting?'

Stevens had answered with the customary phrase. 'You know the trouble with you Yanks. You're overfed, overpaid, oversexed — *and over here!*' He had grinned cheekily as a gigantic paratrooper had towered over him, a beer bottle grasped in his hamlike fist. Before the paratrooper had been able to bring it down on the cockney's head, Lone Star Alamo Jones, the Texan member of the Destroyers, had punched him on the point of the jaw. Thus had started their swift road to the glasshouse, from which 'C' had ordered Crooke and Mallory to free them by any means they could.

Crooke wondered whether the degradations of the Military Prison had had any effect on his men. But their faces revealed nothing. The Destroyers — Stevens, deserter and black marketeer; Peters, the Guardsman, the big ex-company sergeant major in the Coldstreams; Yank, the Texan mercenary and killer; Muhammed, the Egyptian petty thief and peddlar of pornographic pictures; Thaelmann, the hard-bitten ex-Dachau inmate and convinced Communist — all of them seemed as ready as ever for action.

Commander Mallory paid off the French taxi driver at the corner of the blacked-out Avenue Gabrielle, deserted save for a drunken GI slumped in the dark doorway.

'We've got to keep up our security,' he explained to the Destroyers as he waited while the taxi drove off. '"C" is very hot on security on this one. We'll go the rest of the way on foot.'

But if 'C' was concerned with security, the guard at the entrance to the SIS's Paris branch wasn't. A plump, pale-faced sergeant wearing the green flash of the Intelligence Corps on his shoulder, he was fast asleep, his head resting on his chin, a half-empty bottle of looted Wehrmacht *Kognak* standing on the little table next to him and his Sten gun hanging carelessly from the back of his chair. In the corner of the dingy entrance, an old-fashioned pot-bellied stove was going out slowly.

'The British Secret Intelligence Service — always on the alert!' Stevens said maliciously. The sergeant continued to snore softly. Crooke hooked his foot around the leg of the chair and pulled. The chair slipped from under the NCO. He crashed heavily to the floor and woke up spluttering angrily, 'What the hell's going on —?'

He stopped short when he saw the two officers staring down at him. Hastily he sprang to his feet and grabbed for his khaki beret.

'Must have dropped off, sir,' he said thickly.

'Yes,' Mallory said, 'like the sleeping beauty no doubt.' He glanced at the bottle of German brandy. 'Helped by your sleeping potion there.'

'But sir,' the NCO started.

'Forget it,' Mallory snapped. 'Who's the duty officer, sergeant?'

'Only l-l-little me,' a mild voice stuttered from the stairs above them.

The Destroyers turned, startled by that well-remembered stutter. An untidy-looking civilian, dressed in a sloppy tweed jacket and baggy grey flannels, was staring down at them from the gloom of the stairs, a faint mocking smile on his face.

'Philby!' Crooke exclaimed.

'Ye-y-yes,' he stuttered. 'Good to see you again, C-Crooke. Let's see, we last met on that C-Caucasian Fox balls-up, didn't we?'

'Oh yes, I remember all right,' Crooke said coldly. Hastily Mallory butted in. He knew that Crooke and the Destroyers felt that Philby had let them down on the Caucasian mission.

'We need help, Philby. We've just got back from SHAEF Headquarters at Versailles and nobody there seems to know anything about the unit your Chief calls…'

'P-p-project X,' Philby interrupted.

'You know about it?'

'Y-y-yes.' He grinned, but his eyes did not light up. To Mallory, this former *Times* correspondent who had been recruited into the SIS at the outbreak of the war, seemed like a circus clown who put on a separate face for every performance, but whose real features always remained hidden in the company of others.

'I'm the SIS's new representative to the p-project.' He turned to the Intelligence Corps sergeant. 'W-w-will you take these rogues to the mess and get them fed?' He nodded to the Destroyers to follow the NCO. 'Hope you know that the p-p-police all over the UK are looking for y-y-you?'

He waited until they had filed away into the interior of the decrepit building, holding up his pale hand to indicate that the two officers should not speak until the door had closed on the Destroyers and the NCO.

'Security's very hot on this one, you know,' he explained. 'Especially with the Yanks. They've fallen for this c-c-covert stuff, hook, line and sinker. General "Wild Bill" Donovan m-m-must have read too much John Buchan as a k-k-kid. They really like the oblique approach.'

'Come on,' Crooke said menacingly, 'what's this all about? Commander Mallory and I have not risked a court-martial getting my men out of prison at your chief's request in order to be given a lot of double-talk! What is this damned Project X?'

'P-p-pace,' Philby said, in no way shocked, holding up his hand for peace. 'I know about as much as you, very little. All I k-k-know is that it's big — very b-b-big.'

'But where the devil are we going to find out what the mission is?' Mallory asked. '"C" said it's vital we get on with it, but we've already wasted forty-eight hours getting those rogues out of jail and getting here.'

'Where?' Philby echoed his query. 'Why, in the Café Sappho at the Pig Alley.'

'Pig Alley?'

'That's r-r-right. *Pig Alley*, the spiritual home of every war-worn Y-y-yank, Place Pigalle.'

CHAPTER 5

The Sappho was packed with officers from half-a-dozen Allied armies in various stages of drunkenness, dressed in a bewildering variety of winter uniforms. They were entertaining peroxided French blondes with champagne at five pounds a bottle in a small room into which they were crammed like olives in a jar. The noise was terrific. Deep masculine voices shouting in English, French and Polish, punctuated by the giggles of French women who obviously wouldn't be spending that night in their own beds. In fact, Crooke thought as the slim female waiter dressed in a man's dinner jacket showed them to a table, most of the women looked as if they hadn't spent a night in their own beds for a devil of a long time.

'Champagne,' Philby ordered, while the waiter tried to escape from the clutches of a drunken Canadian infantry officer at the next table. He slapped a pile of dirty franc notes on the tablecloth. 'Expenses,' he explained.

Behind them the Canadians from the Fourth Division began to bawl drunkenly,

'And the mate at the wheel had a bloody good feel
At the girl I left behind me!'

Suddenly from the little stage came a clumsy roll on the drums and a slim and attractive middle-aged woman in man's clothes sprang on to the floor with consciously youthful energy. A burst of cheering came from the drunken audience.

'Take it off, lady — take it off!' the Canadians yelled. Mallory looked at Crooke. His face wore an expression of severe disapproval. The Commander took a sip of his champagne and grinned. Crooke was a puritan at heart.

'Ladies and gentlemen,' the woman said in fluent American-English, 'tonight we offer you a spectacle without parallel in Pig Alley.' Flinging back one arm, she cried, 'Ladies and gentlemen, I give you — Sue and Suzette!'

The lights went out and there was another roll on the drums.

As the spotlight came on and bathed the little stage in its dusky light, a voice at Mallory's side said, 'Excuse me, gentlemen.' Crooke and Mallory looked up. An undersized American with the silver eagle of a full colonel on his overseas cap stood there, his eyes hidden by the gleam on the glass of his spectacles. 'I wonder if you've got a bit of room for me?' He hesitated. 'It's very crowded in here and that group over there seems rather rough.'

Mallory was about to refuse when his eyes caught the glint of the silver cross on the officer's lapel. He looked at Crooke. The latter's mouth dropped open slightly. The American was a member of the Corps of Chaplains!

'Why, yes — yes, certainly, padre,' the Commander answered and moving back allowed him to drag up a chair.

'Thank you,' the American began. Suddenly he gasped. The red spot had moved to illuminate two women at the rear of the stage. Both were motionless and both completely naked. The older of the two, her face stamped with hawklike, rapacious, aristocratic dissipation, sat in a straight-backed chair while behind her a young woman was standing attentively, her slim body bronzed, beautiful and gleaming, the nipples of her slight breasts tinted a bright red.

The audience was suddenly very silent. Crooke glanced at his companions. Mallory's and Philby's attentions were directed at the stage. The chaplain's eyes were concealed by his glasses. The bass drum began to beat, its rhythm suggesting the throb of a human pulse, as the young woman reached out a delicate hand and released the golden band that held the other's dyed blue-black hair in place. Using an ivory-backed brush she began to brush it with long languid strokes. For two minutes she continued to do so — softly, systematically, stroke after stroke. Then she stopped and glided noiselessly out of the circle of light, as if she had made a sudden decision.

Very carefully, trying not to make a noise, Crooke took a sip of his champagne. On the stage the older woman sank back in the chair, and thrust her breasts forward voluptuously. Opening her legs slightly, she waited. The beat of the drum increased in tempo. Suddenly Crooke felt the chaplain's hand on his knee. He swung round, his face flushing angrily. In the eerie red light, the chaplain grinned.

'No, I'm not like that, Mr Crooke,' he said, his mild-mannered voice abruptly hard and business-like. 'My name is Perkins. I'm from Project X!'

Crooke nudged Mallory. 'Did you hear that?' he whispered. On the stage the girl returned, padding silently across the floor into the circle, her taut breasts hardly moving. The other woman spoke for the first time.

'Paint me,' she whispered in a hoarse voice.

Lightly the girl dipped a brush into the bright red paint she carried. The woman shivered in anticipation. She drew in her stomach muscles and thrust forward her breasts to receive the first stroke of the brush on her nipples.

A tremor of excitement ran through the audience as Perkins whispered, 'Sorry to have to play games like this, gentlemen, but you'll understand why later. Now listen to this. I'm sending over a deuce-and-a-half to pick up you and your fellows at 0800 tomorrow morning — a two-and-a-half ton truck,' he added, seeing that Crooke did not understand. 'You're to proceed to St Vith in Belgium. It's about seven hours' drive from here at this time of the year.'

On the stage the older woman's stomach glistened. Sweat shone all over her now. Her breath came in quick feverish gasps. But the younger woman continued to paint her body in apparent unawareness. The drum began to crash and roll. Crooke could hear Philby grunting with excitement as he tried to take in the scene and listen to the American at the same time.

'There you'll report to Major Abel,' he was saying, face close to theirs, eyes still hidden behind the glasses. 'He's the commander of the 453rd US Chemical Warfare Company attached to the 106th Infantry Division, which holds that sector of the front.'

The woman's passion had reached climax. From somewhere behind the stage a gramophone had taken over from the drum. Its music was blatant in its sexuality. Her hips began to grind in time to it. A stream of sweat trickled down between her breasts. Jerking her head back and forth, she mouthed unintelligible obscenities. Once her fingers rose and sought the younger woman's breasts but in time she controlled herself and let them fall. The younger woman continued her painting. There was something sadistic in the way she tortured the older woman with her brush, but her face was calm and completely blank of emotion.

'He'll brief you on the latest situation and give you your orders. And remember,' the chaplain added, 'Project X has got the backing of President Roosevelt as well as your own Prime Minister!'

'But what's our mission?' Crooke yelled above the ever mounting noise of the music.

On the stage the older woman's teeth were bared. Her nostrils flared. Sweat was pouring from her now. The music became more frenzied.

'*What?*' Perkins shouted.

'*What's our mission?*' Crooke repeated.

The woman's legs were wide open now. Her belly moved in and out rapidly.

'Come on … come on, grind baby!' the Canadians shouted harshly. Crooke could hear his fellow spectators panting like dogs, the sweat pouring down their excited faces.

The little American brought his mouth closer to Crooke's ear. He shouted something but Crooke still did not catch the words. The music was too loud. On the stage the older woman had lost control of herself completely. Harsh gasps came from her lips and her long skinny fingers formed into claws of enraged lust.

'What did you say?' Crooke bellowed.

'*I said,*' the American roared, his hands cupped around his mouth, '*Abel'll brief you. But this much I'll tell you now — you're going to bring back a bottle of water — a bottle of ordinary Rhine water!*'

Suddenly the older woman threw herself forward and grasped the younger one's breasts. The audience gasped. The girl screamed. In the audience an officer laughed, but the laugh did not ring quite true. Holding onto the girl's breasts, the older woman brought her sweat-lathered face close to hers and hissed through gritted teeth: 'I'm going to screw you — now!'

Then the spotlight went out, leaving the whole place in darkness. When the main lights went on again, the two women had vanished. Save for the abandoned paint brush, there was no sign of their having been there.

The little band began to play again. The audience, suddenly sober, applauded hesitantly. They avoided looking at each other, as if embarrassed. Someone got up to dance. The waiters started to circulate again. Crooke blinked and turned to Perkins. But his seat was empty. The American had vanished as abruptly as he had come.

Philby licked his lips and tried to smile. 'Our cousins from b-b-beyond the sea do like to have their little jokes, don't they?' he stuttered.

CHAPTER 6

The Tech-5 driving the truck hit the brakes again. Another shell-hole pitted the narrow Belgian road. The Destroyers were jolted out of their wooden seats in the back of the truck. Mallory moaned and rubbed his backside. Pulling the brown American Army blanket tighter over his frozen legs, he said weakly, 'I don't think I've ever been stiffer or colder in my life.'

Stevens, whose nose was blue and dripping with the biting cold, attempted a grin. 'Now yer know how the other half lives, sir,' he said. 'Us common folks go through this all the time.' He wiped the back of his hand across his nose.

'And no doubt you deserve it,' Mallory answered grimly.

They relapsed into a miserable silence as the driver accelerated again. They were nearly at the end of their long journey through the icy Belgian countryside, the road pocked with shell-holes, the fields on both sides littered with burnt-out tanks and shattered guns from the fighting of the previous September.

The mud-splattered truck approached the outskirts of St Vith. Through the shattered windows of the houses the Destroyers could see GIs sprawled on the floor. Most of them were asleep, wrapped in their khaki sleeping bags. A few were cleaning weapons or scraping mud off the soles of their combat boots with trench knives.

They looked very young, Mallory thought. Not much more than eighteen, draftees caught in the last scraping of the barrel. But still the Ardennes was a quiet front — known as the 'Ghost Front' — where battered US formations went to rest and new ones to train. Nothing had happened in the well-wooded border area since the Americans first arrived here.

The driver changed down as they took a corner. At the bend four GIs were huddled around an anti-tank gun, dug in the ditch.

'Poor bastards,' the Yank said. They were getting close to the front now. The eternal background music to a battlefield — the rumble of heavy guns — was getting louder and the horizon was a permanent dull pink.

In the back garden of one of the houses a huge German Tiger tank squatted like some dead monster. A hundred yards away in a field sat its opponent, an American Sherman, one track gone and a great hole in its belly. Mallory stared at the tangled mess of wires and what looked like white ribbons running parallel with the road.

'What's the ribbon for?' he asked.

'The engineers string them, sir,' Peters said politely, while the others, scornful at such lack of knowledge, remained silent. 'They show that the verges have been cleared of mines.'

'You hope,' the Yank added cynically, as the truck moved into St Vith's main street, packed with the vehicles of the 106th Infantry Division's HQ and staff officers hurrying from office to office with clipboards under their arms.

A few minutes later the Tech-5 pulled up in front of a tightly shuttered stone house, just behind the onion-towered Baroque church.

'Here you is, Capn sir,' he said. He pointed a finger at the stencilled sign '453 Chemical Warfare Company'. A fresh-faced, freckled PFC, wearing a helmet-liner which was too big for him, opened the door, whistling tonelessly through his front teeth. He stopped and his face lit up as he recognized their uniforms.

'Hi,' he said with apparent enthusiasm, 'you fellers from Paris? From Colonel Perkins?' He waved towards a big pot of coffee on a stove in the corner. 'Help yourselves to some Java while I tell the major you're here.'

'Thanks,' Crooke said. He noticed that the American had never taken his hand away from his pistol holster which he kept tied low to his thigh like a western gun-slinger in the films. Stiffly, the frozen Destroyers picked up the canteen cups lined along the windowsill. The Yank seized the big black pot.

'Real American Joe,' he said. 'Better than all the tea in the world!'

'Major Abel will see you now, sir,' the Private said. Crooke and Mallory put down their cups.

'You chaps relax,' Crooke said. 'I'll brief you later.' The two officers walked into the office and behind them the Private closed the door carefully, still with his hand on his pistol. Major Abel did not rise to greet them, but he waved them to sit down, a welcoming smile on his emaciated features.

'Glad to see you, gentlemen,' he said, and then with a chuckle, 'Surprised Sergeant Perkins managed to drag you out of that fancy dive where he met you.'

'Sergeant?' Mallory said surprised. 'I thought Perkins was a colonel!'

Abel ran his hand through his grey, crew-cut hair and a grin crossed his face.

'In this outfit, Commander, no one is what he seems to be. PFC Schwarz outside, for instance, the pride of the 453rd Chemical Warfare Company. He wouldn't know mustard gas from chilli sauce. In fact, he's a special agent from the FBI on temporary duty with us.'

'To do what, sir?' Crooke asked.

'To guard me, Lieutenant Crooke.' Again Abel chuckled. 'Let me explain. This chemical warfare business is just a cover. Back in Washington, they're always using covers and project names — X or Y or Z. Almost as if they're afraid of letting themselves know what their own secrets are.'

Mallory wondered who 'they' were, but did not interrupt.

'You see, there isn't any company, really. Just me, a driver and Schwarz, my bodyguard. And now you will be wondering what my real job is and why I need a bodyguard to do it. The answer to the bodyguard bit is simple.' He pointed to the dark line of the hills beyond the little border town. 'That's the line and the Germans are up there. They could come down here any night of the week and collar me if they wanted. And my bosses think I know too much to run around loose without a guard.' He paused. 'The answer to the other bit is more complicated. In fact, it's almost the story of my life. But I'll try to make it short, if not sweet. By profession, I'm a college professor — physics is my subject. As a young man I studied in Germany — in Tubingen to be exact. There I got friendly with a serious sort of chap, who was about my own age, called Klaus Schurz. While I was busy chasing Fräuleins, he got buckled down to some serious research.' Again the Major chuckled at the memory. Major Abel did a lot of chuckling, though the laugh never quite rang true.

'Well, in the twenties when things got tough in Germany due to the depression, I managed to wangle a graduate assistantship for Klaus at Harvard. That sort of cemented our friendship and after he went back in 1932 we continued to correspond. In 1938 he was kicked out of his research at the Kaiser Wilhelm Institute in Tubingen. He was half-Jewish. But he was too important to be put into one of those concentration camps we're beginning to hear about. After all, he was one of

Germany's top-flight scientists. So he was given a research job in a factory in the big industrial complex around Leverkusen on the Rhine. And that's where he's still working to this day.'

The Major stopped. Outside a battery of heavy field guns opened with a crash. He looked at his watch.

'Four o'clock on the nose,' he commented. 'The last hate of the day before the 106th Division closes up shop for the night. They're a green bunch. They always start their barrage at the same time. The Germans must be safely tucked away in their foxholes by now.'

'Klaus — your German friend?' Mallory prompted.

'Oh yes. Excuse me. In the Leverkusen area the Germans are doing the Third Reich's must important research and Klaus is in a position to inform us on the state of that research.'

'What kind of research?' Mallory asked.

'Something which could drastically change the whole course of the war in the Germans' favour, if they brought it off. A weapon which they could use to wipe out our entire civilization, Commander Mallory.'

CHAPTER 7

'You see, gentlemen,' Major Abel explained, 'since 1941, both British and American scientists have been working on a new type of explosive. How can I explain it to you in layman's terms?' He bit his lower lip momentarily. 'It's a kind of self-propagating reaction involving neutrons, which could lead to an explosion. Though how big that explosion would be no one knows. Mathematicians worked out last year that it could be anything from zero to the equivalent of 80,000 tons of TNT.' He looked up at them. This time he did not chuckle. 'If the scientists could bring it off, an explosive charge of that kind — just one charge, mark you — could do more damage than all the thousand bombers, carrying six tons of bombs each, that your RAF used in the first big raid on Cologne in 1942 — and you remember what that place looked like afterwards.'

Mallory and Crooke were impressed.

'Yes,' Abel agreed. 'I know what you're thinking.'

'Do you mean that we've got something like that, Major?' Crooke asked, breaking into the sudden heavy silence. Major Abel said severely, 'I'm not authorized to tell you that, Lieutenant Crooke. Besides that is no concern of yours or the 453rd Chemical Warfare Company. Our — rather *your* — problem is Klaus.'

'I see,' Mallory said. 'Please carry on, Major.'

'Well, just before Pearl Harbor I received a letter from Klaus; I hadn't heard from him for a couple of years. In it he told me that he was working close to a factory involved in the production of heavy water. You know what that is?'

The two officers looked blank.

'Well, it's something used in the research I've just told you about. I took it to our authorities and was told that they already knew that the Germans were pursuing the same channels as we were. That's how I got involved in the business — unfortunately. In 1942 and 1943 you British took a hand in trying to knock out the German's potential in this field, especially in Norway. Last year your commandoes put their plant out of operation there, and we kinda forgot the German project. Since this summer, however, and all the talk of V-weapons with more to come, our authorities have not been so sure. The people who run Project X want to know just what the Germans are up to — and quick.'

'That's where we come in, I suppose?' Crooke said.

'Right. You Destroyers have the top security clearance. You're tough and used to clandestine operations. The OSS agents we had available are not in your class. Those Washington canteen commandoes talk too much anyway. We need you to bring back the bottle of water that Sergeant Perkins told you about. You see, Klaus contacted me about fourteen days ago by channels you don't need to know about. He's going to bring the bottle into the frontline area — or at least as far as he dare. You're going to meet him and bring him and the bottle back here.'

'May I ask why the bottle's so important, Major?' Crooke said. 'I have to give my Destroyers some explanation. They're a hard bunch, but they don't like to risk their necks just like that, not knowing why.'

'I understand. Of course, you need to know something. Tell them this. If our people back in Washington can get their hands on that bottle of water, they'll be able to make an educated guess at the state of the German research.' Very deliberately he said, 'Our analysis of the contents of that bottle could well decide the future course of the war. Tell your Destroyers that, Lieutenant Crooke.'

Through the window they could see the red flares in the sky above the hill. Moments later there came the rapid burr of a German machine gun, followed by the obscene belch of a mortar.

'The 106th's taking up the rations to the guys in the line — you know what the GIs say, one guy in the line and five to bring up the Coca-Cola,' Major Abel said and shook his head in dismay. 'Jesus, when they go up there, you can hear them miles away. No wonder the Germans can clobber them every goddamn time.'

For a moment or two they watched the brief firefight on the hillside, the tracer zig-zagging back and forth like angry fireflies. Then the firing gave way to single rifle-shots and finally stopped altogether.

'Okay,' the Major continued. 'This is the deal. Tomorrow, Friday the 15th is Klaus' day off. He's going to take the night train from Cologne to the railhead at Kyllburg.' Without rising he swung round and using his ruler as a pointer, rapped the big wall map behind his desk. 'Here, if he can get through the control point there okay, he's gonna take the local bus to Prüm here.' Again he tapped the map with his ruler. 'And from there on in, he's going to hoof it to Bleialf, which is the headquarters of the People's Grenadier Division holding the line opposite us. According to the 106th's G2, the Division is pretty green and ropey — a lot of young kids recently drafted. At all events our information is that the line is thinly and carelessly held. So we're hoping that Klaus will be able to get within a mile or two of Steinebrück — here.' He gestured towards the window. 'In fact it's not too far beyond the hill there.'

'But Major, that's pretty heavily wooded country up there,' Crooke objected. 'It would be a bit like trying to find a needle in a haystack in that wood.'

'Of course. We've arranged a *treff* — I believe that's what you spy guys call it — with Klaus at a little chapel here. I'll mark the reference on the map I'll give you later. It's one of those places they have a lot of in this area, just enough room to kneel and pray to the Virgin Mary statue inside it. It's the best kind of cover we could give Klaus at such short notice. In case a German patrol comes along, he'll just have to play one of the local peasants getting in a quick prayer before moving on. They're pretty religious around here.' He shrugged. 'Poor, I know, but the best we could do.'

Mallory nodded his agreement but said nothing. For a moment or two Crooke studied the map behind the Major, then he asked, 'And how are we going to recognize this chap Klaus, Major? You know him, of course. Will you be coming along with us?'

The Major shook his head sadly. 'No, Lieutenant Crooke, I'm afraid that I shall not be able to come with you.' Slowly he rose, grasping the edge of his desk with both hands to do so. The bottom half of his right leg was missing and the neatly tucked-in khaki of his slacks was stained a damp black, as if the stump concealed below it was suppurating badly. 'You see, I'm afraid Project X demands strange and painful sacrifices of those who work in it.'

Now the two British officers realized why he had called his entry into the top-secret scheme 'unfortunate'.

CHAPTER 8

The White half-track clattered up the steep, *pavé* road, the long line of trees on both sides stripped white by shellfire, branches lying in the ditches like so many sun-dried bones. On either side the frozen fields were full of gigantic molehills of fresh soil, caused by the morning's shelling.

'We're coming up to the line,' Schwarz said, who was driving the half-track. 'But there's a 106th outpost a couple of klicks further on.'

Crouched at the machine gun above Schwarz, Stevens, now dressed like the rest of the Destroyers in GI uniform, carefully surveyed the fir forests on each side of the little hill-road. With a roar Schwarz changed down.

'All right, fellers,' he yelled, 'this is the end of the line!' He pulled the half-track off the road into a clump of firs and indicated the battered remains of what had once been a forester's cottage perched on a mound some five hundred yards away. 'That's it. That's the 106th's first line of defence.'

'Cor love a duck!' Stevens said. 'Would you believe it!' Crooke knew what was going through their heads. The defensive position stuck out like a sore thumb; it was such an obvious place for an outpost that even the newest recruit would have avoided it.

The young GIs with the golden lion patch of the 106th on their shoulders crouched in puddles of mud on the rubble-strewn floor of the cottage. In one corner their bedding was piled next to a wooden ration box covered with the remains of their midday meal. The 19-year-old sergeant in charge was as dirty and as bearded as his men — and as scared. He took out the combat knife from the side of his boot and pointed vaguely to the green mass of firs to their front.

'The Germans are up there somewhere,' he said nervously.

'But where, sergeant?' Crooke asked, trying to control his anger.

'Hell, I don't know,' the NCO shrugged his shoulders. 'A guy can get killed out there.'

'But don't you run any patrols?' Crooke persisted.

'Are you kidding?' a dark-skinned PFC said angrily. 'This war is nearly over and Mrs Ricci's boy ain't figuring to earn his mom a golden star.'

'Knock it off,' the Yank snarled and hitched up his Browning automatic rifle more comfortably. 'You guys'll have me creaming my drawers in a minute.'

'Say, you're not a limey!' Ricci said swinging round. 'You're an American.'

'Yeah,' the Texan drawled, 'but not a goddamn chicken…'

'All right,' Crooke snapped, 'that's enough!' Turning to Schwarz, he said, 'Get back to the half-track and stand by there. Radio your chief and Commander Mallory that we're moving out.'

The ex-FBI agent nodded. 'Roger, Lieutenant.'

A few minutes later the Destroyers moved off into the fir forest with Ricci jeering behind them, 'You'll regret it!'

'And he will be regretting it, too,' Muhammed whispered to Stevens in his stilted English as they plodded up the hill in single file. He held up the carton of Lucky Strikes which he had palmed as they left the ruined cottage.

Stevens shook his head in mock sorrow. Muhammed grinned showing a mouthful of gleaming teeth. 'Good for black market. Plenty of girls —'

'Quiet back there!' Crooke hissed.

The forest was dark, with the dull December light cut out effectively by the tightly-packed firs that marched up the steep hillside like rank after rank of Prussian soldiers. But in spite of the tough going, Crooke avoided the tracks. He knew the Germans would have them covered by fixed fields of fire. They plunged into the undergrowth, working themselves into a sweat in a matter of minutes, fighting for breath as the going got increasingly steeper.

'Christ, this is a right bugger!' Stevens cursed softly as he stumbled once again. 'What the hell do they think we are — sodding goats!'

'It looks like it,' Peters gasped as he wiped the sweat off his brow.

It was almost dusk when they reached the map reference which Major Abel had given them. Crooke raised his hands and let them fall. Gratefully the Destroyers flopped down on the frozen earth. Crooke strained his eye, trying to penetrate the green gloom ahead. There was no movement save the gentle swaying of the firs and the soft rustle of the icy wind in their tops. Now he realized why Abel had picked this spot as a rendezvous with his German contact. It seemed hardly possible that the greatest war in history was being fought in the neighbourhood. He could easily believe the tales he had heard back in England of German soldiers slipping back through the dense woods to meet their former Belgian girlfriends. The 'Ghost Front' was an ideal place for clandestine operations.

Crooke rose to his feet again and, stretching out his arms, brought them forward in an arc. The Destroyers knew what he meant. They picked up their weapons and, rising, spread out in a line. Slowly and alertly they began to move forward, putting their feet down with exaggerated care.

Suddenly there was a faint noise in the trees to their front. They stopped immediately. The trees rustled again. Whoever was out there was hesitant, as if he did not quite know where he was. Then the sound stopped again. Somewhere out there the unknown person had stopped and was lurking among the trees — waiting.

The minutes passed as they crouched there tensely, but nothing happened and the sound had stopped completely. In the end Crooke decided to act. He signalled the Yank to come closer.

'Jones,' he whispered, 'you're coming with us. Cover us with the BAR.' He turned to Thaelmann. 'You stick with me. I might need you to interpret.'

With a quick wave of his hand he indicated that the rest should take cover, then moved off with Thaelmann. Behind them the Yank advanced, the automatic rifle pressed tightly against his hip, ready for action.

Crooke could not overcome his feeling of fear. There was something eerie, almost uncanny, about the forest. It reminded him of his days in the desert before the war when he had been able to sense the presence of wandering Bedouins even when they were still miles away. In the trees someone was waiting for them — that he knew. But whether that someone was enemy or friend was anybody's guess. He brushed aside a fallen fir to reveal the grey stone outline of one of the typical rural *Marterln* of the area.

'The chapel,' he whispered to Thaelmann. Slowly, very slowly, he raised his body above the frozen undergrowth, careful not to present a target for any waiting German soldier with an itchy finger. He nudged Thaelmann who called softly, '*Sind Sie das?*'

There was no answer but the soft rustle of the wind.

Crooke bit his lip. He knew he couldn't wait much longer. As soon as it was dark, the Germans would be pushing out their recce patrols as they always did just after nightfall. He had to make a decision one way or another.

'All right,' he whispered, gripping his American Colt tighter in his sweating fist. 'I'm going forward. Come on.' He beckoned to the Yank to follow up.

Cautiously they crept towards the little chapel. As they came closer, Crooke made out the faded carving of Jesus on the cross which hung from its side. Suddenly he stopped. A dark figure was crouched below it. It was a man, on his knees below the cross as if in silent prayer.

'Klaus Schurz?' he asked. The man did not reply. Crooke glanced to left and right. The little glade was empty and, taking a chance, he ran out into the open. The man, almost hidden by the gloom of the chapel wall, did not move.

Thaelmann brushed by Crooke. '*Mensch*,' he hissed urgently, '*was ist mit Ihnen los?*' Still the man did not reply.

Thaelmann grabbed him roughly by the shoulder. 'I asked you something!'

Slowly the kneeling man toppled over, his sightless eyes staring into nothing. His hands were not clasped in prayer; they were claws of agony trying to wrench out the bayonet which had been thrust deep into his chest. Klaus Schurz was dead.

CHAPTER 9

'Bloody hell!' Stevens said in awe, as he stared down at the dead German lying by the wall of the chapel, his blood already beginning to congeal in the freezing air. 'Who did that?' But none of the Destroyers could tell him. Open-mouthed, they stared at the murdered agent. Then Crooke pulled himself together. He knew they had to get out of the wood — and quick.

'Peters and Yank — over there smartish — and keep your eyes peeled!' While they doubled to carry out his orders, he knelt down by the body of the shabbily-dressed German and ran his hands over his body. His pockets contained very little. 'Identity card,' Thaelmann explained as Crooke handed the documents one by one to him. 'Pass freeing him from military duty. Ration card — heavy worker's scale, train ticket, Cologne–Kyllburg.'

'Damn!' Crooke cursed, rising to his feet. 'Where the hell's the bottle?'

'Here, sir.' It was Muhammed. As always he had been nosing around the chapel 'finding stuff, before it gets goddamn lost', as the Yank had complained.

'Where?'

Muhammed pointed a long finger at the row of artificial flowers lining the top of the little stone altar, each bunch in a differently shaped bottle.

'How do you know which is his bottle?' Crooke asked. Time was running out fast. They had to get out of the chapel quickly. Muhammed picked up one of them, dropped the dusty paper flowers to the floor near the dead man's head and passed it over. Crooke took the bottle carefully, avoiding spilling any of the liquid it contained. He looked at it curiously. 'This one?'

'Yessir,' Muhammed said eagerly, flashing his teeth. 'Look at the label. You are seeing — Schnapps?'

Crooke nodded. Still he did not understand what the Destroyer was getting at.

'Well, sir, would religious persons be putting flowers in a holy place in a bottle of hot water?'

'Firewater,' Stevens corrected him automatically. He peered over Crooke's shoulder. 'It's the only one with a German label, sir. *Koeln am Rhein*,' he read the German name for Cologne slowly. 'Them others is all Belgian. Muhammed must be right, sir.'

Crooke nodded. Grasping the bottle, he turned the screw cap firmly and stowed it carefully inside his jacket. 'Let's hope you two rogues are right. Come on. We're going back.'

The Destroyers began to move down the hillside, the Yank and Peters bringing up the rear, their weapons at the ready. Outside the chapel the body of Klaus Schurz began to stiffen rapidly in the icy cold.

They ran into the ambush five minutes after Schwarz had reversed the half-track and begun driving them down the road which led to St Vith.

There was a soft hiss as a bright white light climbed into the night sky. It exploded with a crack directly above them and bathed them in an icy blue light.

'Flare,' Thaelmann yelled.

Schwarz put his foot down and the White shot forward. Crouched over the wheel, he forced the cumbersome vehicle round the tight bend at fifty miles an hour. The flare started to descend and Crooke breathed out in relief. They were going to make it. Then it happened. There was an explosion close by. A flurry of sparks rose from the ditch some twenty yards away. Metal struck metal with a resounding blow. The half-track reeled. Schwarz's face shot forward and hit the armour plate with a crash. As hot metal pattered against the side of the White, it careered against a tree, bounced off, completely out of control and smashed into the ditch on the left-hand side of the narrow road.

For a moment no one moved. Then Stevens at the machine gun fired a long burst in the direction from which the shot had come.

'*Panzerfaust!*' Crooke yelled. He grabbed Schwarz by the shoulder. His eyes were wide open and staring. Blood was pouring thickly from his smashed face.

'Schwarz,' he cried. There was no answer. The American was dead. Gently he let him fall to the steering wheel again. 'Come on — bail out,' he roared above the clatter of cartridge cases tumbling all around him. 'Let's get out of this.'

Crooke dropped to the ground. The White's left track was flopped across the road. Oil was pouring from the fractured axle. He fired six shots into the wood as his men got out of the stricken vehicle. A machine gun started to chatter from that direction, but its fire was erratic and wide of the mark.

Crooke dropped into the ditch. 'Let's get out of here before that gunner zeroes in on us.'

On hands and knees they crept down the frozen ditch while the machine gun sought them, the bullets harmlessly cutting the foliage above their heads. Five minutes later they emerged, slapping their hands and knees free from dirt, the sounds of the ambush dying away behind them.

Now the stars had come out. In their frosty light they saw the first flakes of snow come drifting gently down, as they hurried along the side of the road. The front seemed to have gone to sleep again. There was no sound now save that of the wind and the soft drift of the snow.

'Do you know where we are, sir,' Peters asked, wiping the snow from his face.

'Not exactly, Peters. But we should be near that hamlet we passed going up to the 106th outpost.'

'Bloody well hope so, sir,' Stevens said. 'Freeze a brass monkey's off tonight.'

We'll be lucky if we're not a lot colder before this night's over, Crooke thought, but he said nothing.

It was about thirty minutes later when they entered the hamlet which was part of the US Infantry Division's front. Cautiously they approached the first house, weapons at the ready. Then they relaxed. The well-remembered voice of the BBC announcer John Snagge was saying: 'This morning Supreme Allied Command stated that Allied troops had made considerable progress in their attempts…'

Crooke opened the door. A hissing Coleman lamp illuminated the little room — a map on the wall covered with red and blue crayon, a kettle steaming on the pot-bellied Belgian stove, the radio, powered by the gasoline generator outside, tuned to the BBC.

'Hello,' he said hesitantly, 'anyone there?' There was no answer save Snagge announcing that Major Glenn Miller had been reported missing while on a flight over the Channel to entertain American troops in France.

The Destroyers, crowding behind him, looked at each other in bewilderment.

'What do you make of it, sir?' Peters asked.

Crooke shrugged. 'I don't know.'

Muhammed shivered. 'It's very strange, sir. The stiffened one up on the hill — and now no one being here.' The Yank strode over to the radio and switched it off. 'Aw, them chicken 106 guys have bugged out! Hell, they was ready to cream their pants as soon as they saw a German!'

'Could be,' Crooke agreed. 'Stevens and Muhammed, get outside and have a scout around. See if you can find anybody.' He sucked his bottom lip. The silence was treacherous. He had the unpleasant feeling that something was going on in the Ardennes — something decidedly unpleasant. 'Listen,' he said to the others as they poked around the abandoned room, 'I don't know exactly how to explain this, but I have a funny feeling that we're in for trouble. What, I don't know; but the balloon's up — I can feel it in my bones.'

'You're right enough there, sir.' It was Stevens. He was standing at the door, with a small, pale GI, wearing steel-rimmed glasses and bare-headed, peering over his shoulder. 'We've just found him.' He jerked his thumb at the American, who was obviously terrified out of his wits.

'Yes sir, hiding in a ditch he was, trembling like a cabbage,' Muhammed added, a box of looted American C rations tucked under his arm.

'Who are you?' Crooke demanded. 'What's your unit?'

'Four twenty-second Infantry, sir,' the little man stuttered. 'Name of Weed — Joe Weed.'

'Yeah, and you just goddamn look like it,' the Yank said contemptuously, as he saw how the little GI's hands trembled.

'Shut up,' Crooke snapped. 'Muhammed close that door and get in here. You don't want to advertise to the Germans that we're here. Now then,' he addressed Weed again, 'what is this? What are you doing here and where's the rest of your unit?'

The GI wiped the back of his dirty hand across his mouth. 'What am I doing here, sir — gee, I'd like to know that myself. Two months ago I was a cook in Metz. Then the head shirt says they need riflemen in the line.' He shrugged. 'So I'm a rifleman. They give me a couple of weeks' training in a ripple-dipple and then they send me up here.'

'I see,' Crooke said. 'But what happened here tonight?'

'Search me, sir. I was on duty all day, so I decided to get some sack-time early — say about five. When I woke up, everybody had gone — all the guys. Can yer believe it? Just gone and left me in the sack without telling me.' He shrugged again. 'With buddies like that a guy don't need enemies.'

'Then what did you do?'

'I went to look for them, sir. I wasn't gonna stay up here by myself.' He shuddered. 'Hell, it's scary. So I started hoofing it back down to St Vith.' And then it came out. 'But the woods are full of Germans, sir! *They're everywhere. Hundreds of the bastards!*

CHAPTER 10

Five minutes later they set off, with Peters in the lead. Crooke followed behind him, accompanied by the ex-cook, who said that he knew a path branching off from the cobbled road, which could take them into St Vith — if they were lucky and no Germans had discovered it!

The night-time silence had taken on a new character, it seemed to Crooke, as they marched stolidly down the road. It had a strange brooding quality which gave him the eerie sensation that someone was just behind him. Twice he fought the desire to look behind him — and lost both times. He shuddered and tried to take his mind off the uncanny silence. He looked up at the night sky. It was hard and bright with stars. To the east there seemed to be a lot of activity. Flares were rising like shooting stars. But the rumble of the heavy artillery had died away almost to nothing.

They cleared the hamlet. The only sign of the infantry position which had occupied the place a couple of hours beforehand was a ration trailer abandoned in the middle of the road, C-ration boxes strewn everywhere.

'Hell, they must have bugged out in one big hurry,' the Yank commented. They marched on, their rubber-soled American combat boots making virtually no sound on the cobbles. Suddenly Peters stopped.

'Hit the deck!' he whispered urgently. The Destroyers dropped immediately. Beside him, Crooke could hear the ex-cook's breath coming hard and fast. The man was scared out of his wits.

Crooke crawled forward, Colt in his fist.

'What is it?'

'There's somebody up there in front of us. Listen, sir.' He screwed his head round so that he could hear better, Crooke did the same. He could hear faint voices. Crooke strained his eye. Suddenly he saw a dark shape move across a gap. He nudged the Guardsman. Softly Peters clicked off his safety catch while Crooke edged his way back to where Thaelmann was lying in a ditch. He brought his mouth close to the German's ear.

'Try them in your language.' Raising himself, Thaelmann called softly, '*Bist du das Willy?*' The reply was immediate and angry.

'*Mensch, halt die Schnauze!*'

The Destroyers looked at each other. The little GI was right. The road to St Vith was blocked. Crooke signalled his men to fall in on him. They scuttled back.

'We'll doss down here in the ditch till just before dawn,' he whispered. 'If it's anything else,' he touched the precious bottle underneath his jacket, 'well then…' But he never finished his sentence. Weed beat him to it.

'God alone can help us,' he said in a voice that was barely under control.

Crooke awoke at 5.30 precisely on that 16 December morning. For the remaining years of life that remained to him he would never forget that dawn.

Abruptly all along the front, the dawn stillness was broken by a tremendous barrage. Hundreds, perhaps thousands, of guns opened fire simultaneously. Thousands of shells sped through the sky, their separate noises merging into one great baleful scream — a terrifying man-made cyclone. Even as he started up from the bottom of the ditch, Crooke knew that that which he had feared was now happening.

With shocked faces they stared at each other, as the shells roared over their heads to their targets in the American line. A shot landed twenty yards away and fragments of hot steel hissed through the air. With their hands pressed over their ears they hugged the ground, feeling it quake beneath them with every fresh salvo.

Then suddenly the great barrage stopped. Not just gun after gun, but every gun at the same time, as if some god had raised his hand in command and ordered them to cease their blasphemous roar. Coughing and spluttering, the Destroyers staggered to their feet. In the echoing silence they brushed the dirt from their uniforms. Stevens said, 'What the bloody hell was that in aid of?'

'Can't you guess?' Crooke snapped, staring round anxiously at the swirling fog that was beginning to roll down the hillside. 'That wasn't an ordinary fighting patrol we bumped into last night. That was the first attack wave.'

'You mean that bloody barrage was to support them?' the Yank said.

'Yes. They…' From the direction of St Vith the burr of a Spandau machine gun cut short his words, followed seconds later by the cries of men going into the attack. A firefight broke out somewhere in the fog.

'Yer right, sir,' Peters said, 'somebody's catching a proper packet down there. So what do we do now?'

'Well, it's obvious we can't get through to St Vith. The Germans will be through the 106th's first line of defence like a hot knife through butter — the Americans are too damn green. As soon as the first wave is through, they will send in the next lot. They'll be confident that their pals have cleared up all resistance, so they'll be careless. We're going to use that carelessness to our advantage.'

'How do you mean?'

'Instead of trying to go back down there, we'll go forward *through them*. Once we're through them, we'll double back and probe their front until we can find a weak spot where we can slip through without any trouble.' He jerked his thumb at the crackle and flash below them. 'We certainly won't find any weak spot down there.'

The woods seemed full of white-uniformed Germans. More than once they were just saved from capture by the fog, escaping in a burst of machine-gun fire. But the tracks, which advancing infantry usually avoided, where no better. The enemy was present there too, in full strength. Every last forest trail seemed to have its column of German armour or motorized infantry advancing nose-to-tail, lights ablaze, secure from Allied air attack by the dense fog. To the harassed Destroyers, it seemed as if the Germans had broken through the American front everywhere in the Ardennes and were advancing into Belgium at breakneck speed, regardless of their losses.

In the early afternoon Crooke was forced to let his men have a break. Weed had developed a bad limp and was protesting that they should head downhill again since they must have broken through the German second line of attack by now.

In the miserable silence they huddled together in the shelter of a grove of dank pines, cold and tired, shivering in the icy wind which seemed to blow directly from Siberia. Muhammed broke out the C-rations which he had found in the abandoned hamlet and they munched the tasteless ham and egg composite. Finally, Crooke pulled out the map Abel had given him and unfolded it.

'This is roughly where we are now,' he said, 'somewhere between Steinebrück and Schönberg. All morning we've been following this ridge. My guess is that we're well behind the German line now. The ridge must have been their jumping off point. I suggest we decide on a line of march and press on till we hit the Americans.'

The suggestion seemed to please Weed.

'That's a good idea, Lieutenant,' he said enthusiastically. 'I'm about pooped. But I guess I could make it if we hike *down*hill.'

The Yank looked at him contemptuously. 'Aw, knock it off, Weed,' he snarled. 'I'm gonna cry my eyes out in a minute!' He turned to Crooke, 'But where are we gonna find our line? Where's the one zero six?' Crooke nodded, as if he had anticipated the question.

'A good point, Jones. My guess is that if the 106th is holding out at all, it will try to maintain the road junctions. Off the roads there's not much room for troops or vehicles to manoeuvre. The valleys are too tight and there's too much forest. The road junctions are vital if the Americans are going to stop the enemy.'

'That stands to reason, sir,' Peters said, 'but where?' Crooke put his finger on the map.

'Here — at Schönberg. You remember when we came up we passed through it. There was a big American communications centre there, which they wouldn't want to abandon in a hurry.'

'And the roads coming in from Germany meet there,' Weed added. Crooke looked at the little PFC curiously.

'How did you know that, Weed?'

Weed shrugged. 'I don't know, Lieutenant. Guess I must have seen it on a map or something.'

Crooke dismissed his suspicion. He got to his feet and tapped his jacket to ensure that the precious bottle was still there.

'All right. On your feet, lads. Let's get going. We've got about three hours before it gets dark and I want to be in Schönberg before then.'

CHAPTER 11

Doggedly the Destroyers ploughed downhill through the driving snow. The few flakes of the previous day had heralded the first heavy snowfall of the winter, which was transforming the dark green of the forests into gleaming white wasteland. Now the sounds of battle were getting closer again. From their front came the rapid burr of machine guns, punctuated by the crackle of rifle fire and the heavy thump of the mortars.

They had just crossed a relatively broad trail, probably used by the loggers before the war, when Crooke held up his hand in warning. He turned his head to the wind.

'Motors,' he whispered. Hardly daring to breathe, the Destroyers listened to the faint steady rumble.

'Tank motors,' Stevens broke in, 'and they're not moving. Down in the hollow there.' Crooke nodded. The tanks were obviously parked, motors idling because of the icy cold, around the bend. The question was — were they German? Peters solved the problem for them a moment later.

'They're not German, sir.'

'How do you know?'

'All the German tanks have diesel motors. Them round the bend are petrol-driven. Might be Yankee Shermans. All their tanks have petrol motors.'

'All right, there's only one way to find out. Spread out. We'll come in through the trees. Yank, you cover me. Weed, you follow me up.'

They pushed on until they were overlooking the tank laager. Three white-painted hulks were parked in the glade, their motors humming steadily. A few yards away from them five men were huddled around a petrol fire, warming their frozen bands. Crooke wiped the snowflakes off his face again and grinned at the Yank.

'Shermans,' he said. 'They're Yanks.'

'Take it easy, sir,' Weed whispered. 'Sometimes the Germans use captured GI equipment.'

'You're right, Weed. Let's get a little closer and have a look at them.'

Together the three men began to creep down the slippery slope towards the tankers crouched round the fire. Once they stopped and tried to make out their conversation, but the wind and the steady rumble of the motors were too loud. Suddenly the Yank stood upright and slung his BAR over his shoulder.

'Hi you guys,' he cried, cupping his hands round his mouth. 'Don't shoot!' 'They're in GI uniform,' he called to Crooke. The men around the fire jerked violently. Their hands flashed down to their pistols as the Yank came floundering down the snowy hillside towards them.

'Don't shoot, guys,' he bellowed. 'We're friends! Got cut off by the Germans!'

The tankers relaxed. Crooke felt a wave of relief flood through his frozen body. He got up and knocked the snow off his soaked pants. Behind him the rest of the Destroyers began to come out of the firs. A couple of the tankers got up and came to meet them. One of them, a big blond Tech-5, who looked as if he hadn't shaved for a couple of days, cried, 'Which of you is the doctor…'

He never finished his sentence. A head emerged from one of the turrets. It was clad in a floppy black beret. Crooke stopped in his tracks. The Yanks did not wear berets: the Germans did!

Surprisingly it was Weed who reacted first. Instantly he flopped down in the snow. With casual skill, he fired without taking aim. His first bullet caught the big blond German in the stomach. He staggered, his hands clutching his belly. Then he pitched forward — dead! At once hell broke loose. Above them on the hillside the other Destroyers dropped into the snow and fired a wild volley at the tankers. Their bullets went wild, but they served their purpose. Frantically the Germans in US uniform scattered for cover.

Then the Yank went into action. Crouching low, legs apart, he fired from the hip. One of the Germans running for the cover of the second tank clapped a hand to his face and skidded to a stop. Slowly he sank to the snow. Another screamed, '*Mein Gott!*' He fell without another sound.

'*Look out!*' Weed yelled. '*The first tank!*' Crooke saw the new danger immediately. The man in the floppy beret was hand-cranking the turret in their direction. Perhaps the electrical system was defective. Crooke did not know. All he knew was that the 76mm was bearing down on them menacingly.

'Come on,' Crooke cried, springing to his feet. 'Let's get the devil out of here!'

Scrambling to their feet they began to run clumsily up the hill through the snow. The great tank-gun fired. A shell roared through the trees, seemingly only inches above their heads. Crooke was lifted off his feet and dashed to the ground. Yards in front of him, the shell exploded. The blast hit him in the face like a flabby fist. All the breath was knocked out of him. His nostrils filled with bitter, acrid smoke. He fought for breath and struggled to his feet shakily.

Behind him tendrils of smoke drifted from the gun muzzle. Inside the turret the gunner would be scrambling frantically to reload. He glanced at the slope ahead of him, with the long, black mark of the shell disfiguring the purity of the snow. The Destroyers lay scattered everywhere, blown over by the blast.

Had they been hit? It seemed impossible that the gun could have missed at that range! But they were up again, fighting their way groggily up the hill. Crooke followed and just as they gained the crest, the tank gunner fired again. But his aim was wide. The only result of his shot was to blow them over the crest into the deep snow on the other side. Moments later they were running blindly into the heart of the forest, blundering through the firs, Crooke in their rear, the fragment of the blond man's question racing through his mind: 'Which of you is the doctor…?'

They slumped, panting, in the snow, their backs against the firs, their chests heaving. In spite of the cold, beads of sweat stood out on their brows. Crooke stared at his Destroyers.

They were beat. The last twenty-four hours were beginning to take their toll. Surprisingly enough, Weed was standing up to the strain better than any of them. Squatting in the snow, he was playing with what he called his 'Mickey Mouse' watch. When he pressed a button a large pointer swung round the dial while the watch gave off the strains of *Who's Afraid of the Big Bad Wolf?*

'For Chrissake,' Stevens groaned, 'can't you turn that sodding thing off, mate! It's getting on me wick.'

'Sorry, buddy,' Weed said and put it carefully away. 'You limeys are touchy folk. I kinda thought you were all stiff-upper-lip and that sort of stuff.'

'You know what thought did, mate,' Stevens said sourly. 'He shat hissen.' Weed smiled, in no way offended.

'Limey humour,' he commented and taking off his glasses wiped them free of snow. He looked up at Crooke, blinking a little without his spectacles. 'I forgot to ask, Lieutenant: how come you Limeys are dressed up in GI duds?'

Unlike most Americans Crooke had met, he pronounced the rank in the British fashion: *'lef-tenant'*, and not *'loo-tenant'*. There was certainly something strange about this mild-mannered GI, Crooke could not help thinking. He was obviously in good physical shape and he had been quick off the mark back at the scene of their encounter with the German tankers. If it hadn't been for him, they might well be making their way to some German POW cage now — or even worse. Crooke had the impression of a man who had been underestimated throughout his life; a competent actor who was now using all the technical knowhow at his disposal to make the best of a pretty poor role.

'It's a long story,' Crooke said.

'Ay, they're all long stories for the bloody Destroyers,' Peters said, his native Geordie accent coming through stronger than usual. Crooke realized that his men were at the end of their tether; they needed a shot in the arm if they were going to get up again in a few minutes' time and plod on to the American lines.

'Well you see, Weed,' he said, raising his voice so that all of them could hear, 'we're on a special mission. We had to penetrate the German lines to get this.' He undid his jacket and carefully took the bottle out. 'I suppose you think that a bit funny, to risk our lives for a bottle of Rhine water, because that is what it contains — ordinary river water! But it's worth it, that I can tell you.' He held it up so that they could all see it clearly. 'This bottle of water is worth more than the whole River Thames at the moment.'

'Why?' Weed asked.

'Because the analysis of that water will tell our scientists whether the Germans are as close as we are to the greatest secret weapon of the war.'

'And what do they call that weapon, sir?' Weed asked.

'I'm told they call it — the atom bomb,' Crooke said.

'The atom bomb,' Weed chuckled. 'That's a helluva funny name for a bomb, ain't it, sir?'

Crooke did not answer. Unconsciously, Weed took out the cheap, nickel watch and pressed the button. The arm swung round and it gave off the faint tinny strains of *Who's Afraid of the Big Bad Wolf?* yet again.

Thirty minutes later, as they emerged from the snowy gloom of the firs to cross a forest trail, they bumped into the thirty-strong fighting patrol of the 99th Infantry Division. They had hit the US line.

CHAPTER 12

A leathery-faced infantry Major watched them wolf down the hot food, like a good mother happy that her brood had such excellent appetites. In the corner of the room, which stank of kerosene, a signaller sat bent over his radio, rapping out the same phrases over and over again: *'This is Sunray. Big brother on its way. Do you read me? Big brother on its way... This is Sunray.'*

Outside the shattered château headquarters of the 2nd Battalion the dispatch riders came and went, roaring through the mud of the courtyard into the night beyond. But in spite of the urgency of his battalion's situation, Major Ross let them eat in silence, breaking it only to order his personal guard to bring them more coffee. Finally, with an appreciative belch, the Yank pushed aside his tin plate, wiped his mouth on his sleeve and sighed contentedly: 'Jesus, Major, I never thought that beans and franks could taste so damn good!'

Major Ross smiled and pushed an open pack of cigarettes across the table. 'Have a "Lucky", soldier.'

Yank nodded his thanks but declined. Muhammed, however, his mouth full of bread and sausage, reached out his skinny hand and took the whole pack.

The Major smiled. 'Does me good to see folks enjoy food like that,' he said.

'Yes, Major,' Stevens replied, sopping up the remains of his food with a piece of bread, 'it might. But it did my belly a lot more good.'

'All right, that's enough,' Crooke interrupted. 'Now then Major, you want to know what's going on out there, don't you?'

Ross nodded. 'You betcha, Lieutenant. The patrol you bumped into in the woods had strict orders not to return until they had a German prisoner. Back here we're desperate for information. And Division's screaming for it.' He pointed to the big wall map, covered with a rash of blue and red marks. 'The Germans seem to be everywhere. As far as we see the situation at this moment, they've broken through our front between here and Monschau. Sixty klicks or more.'

Crooke whistled. 'That much! So this is a major offensive?'

'You'd better believe it! Let's face it — those kids of the 106th up front just panicked. Most of them have bought it as far as we can make out. But as the brass says,' he added ruefully, 'the situation is fluid — goddamn fluid.'

'Well, this is what we saw on our way down here.' Quickly and expertly Crooke sketched in their experiences of the last twenty-four hours, using his map to fill in the references as far as he knew them. Then he and the Destroyers sat silent while the Major took over the radio himself and signalled the latest information to the Divisional Commander.

He came back with a respectful smile on his face. 'The Commanding General's compliments,' he said. 'He thanks you for the information and asks me to inform you that he'll be sending his own private plane to pick you up at first light. You folks must have plenty of pull with the big brass. Boy, to be able to get the general's plane — just like that!' He clicked his fingers together smartly.

Crooke smiled. 'When's first light?'

'Can't be sure. The forecast is low ceiling and bad visibility. Hell, everybody else is grounded! But the Commanding General got his orders to have you picked up direct from SHAEF. And some guy called Commander Mallory, or something like that, sends his regards.'

'*Mallory?*' Crooke sat up suddenly.

'Yeah, something like that. I thought it was an Irish name.'

'*Commander Mallory!*' Stevens exclaimed. 'I knew he wouldn't be caught with his pants down! Got out, after all. Good for the Senior Service!'

Major Ross looked at them as if they had all suddenly gone mad. Then he said, 'Gentlemen, I've got work to do. But there are plenty of empty cots in the next room. If you can stand the din of our battery of attached Long Toms which are going to clobber the Germans in exactly five minutes, you're sure welcome to them.'

'Me too, Major?' Weed asked timidly.

'Sure, son. Why not? We'll send you up to one of the rifle companies in the morning. Hit the hay now.'

The Destroyers needed no urging. Five minutes later they were all asleep. The opening roar of the bombardment did not even occasion a stir.

Crooke was scraping off two days' growth of beard when the light plane arrived and by the time he had finished the pilot was already surrounded by the other Destroyers. He shook hands with the pilot, a brash young man in a leather jacket, and was told that they would be taking off almost immediately. 'As soon as I can grab a cup of Joe and get gassed up, we'll take off, sir.'

Crooke was amused by the 'sir'. Although the pilot looked all of twenty-one, he was already a major and outranked him by two grades. 'Fine,' he said, 'I'll get my jacket and have some coffee myself.' He looked around the room. 'Where's Weed?'

'He's in the bog, sir,' Stevens said. 'He said that yesterday's do upset his stomach.'

Crooke nodded. 'Just thought I'd say goodbye to him. After all he got us out of a bit of mess yesterday. In spite of your doubts about his courage, Jones,' he added pointedly.

The Yank said nothing.

Five minutes later they followed the pilot out onto the snowy field at the back of the chateau. Two GI's, carbines slung over their shoulders, were standing by the prop of the plane ready to swing it.

The pilot nodded to them as he swung himself into the cockpit. 'Okay,' he yelled, 'let's get her on the road!'

The two GI's swung the prop with all their strength and the engine roared into life.

Crooke cast a last glance behind him. Weed must still be in the bog. He shrugged. They would have to leave without a goodbye. 'Okay, Muhammed, you're first.'

Muhammed's face went green. He was scared stiff of flying. Stevens poked the butt of his carbine in his back. 'Come on, get yer finger out!'

Muhammed reached up to climb into the cabin. But he never made it. With an ear-splitting roar a plane came zooming in from the east. At over three hundred miles per hour it sped along the field at barely a hundred feet, little red flames crackling from its wings. As it flashed over their heads, the Destroyers caught a glimpse of the black and white crosses painted on its wings.

At the same moment Crooke saw the little plane lift off the ground. It crashed down almost at once and disappeared in a cloud of thick black smoke. When it cleared he saw that the undercarriage was shattered; yellow flames were beginning to lick along the length of its fuselage.

He started to run to the pilot's aid but the Focke-Wulf came screaming in again. From somewhere behind the château a machine gun started to fire. The Focke-Wulf roared upward in a steep climb. Seconds later it vanished into the low cloud.

The General's plane was completely wrecked. It lay at a crazy angle, one wing crumpled up, a line of machine-gun bullet holes down the length of its fuselage. Peters wrenched open the door. The pilot lay slumped over the controls in the smashed confusion of the cockpit. He did not move when Peters touched him on the shoulder. Carefully Peters raised his body. His face was no longer handsome. In its centre there was a red gaping hole. Peters lowered him gently and, turning to the rest of the Destroyers, poked his thumb downwards. 'He's had it,' he said.

Slowly they walked back to the château while the excited HQ personnel ran on to the field to examine the wreck of the General's plane.

'What now, sir?' Thaelmann broke the silence.

'We'll have to wait for some other kind of transport,' Crooke said absently. Suddenly he stopped and looked at them. 'Don't you think it's strange?' he asked.

Stevens, always quicker on the uptake than the rest of them, nodded. 'You mean the plane, sir?'

'Yes. How do you account for the appearance of that Focke-Wulf just like that? Was it merely chance? A German plane coming in out of the blue just as we're going to —' his voice faded away.

'Yeah,' Stevens said. 'It would be worth risking that kite to stop us taking off. Or better still to kill us while we were sitting ducks out there in the plane. That would have been a nifty way of putting an end to our mission.'

'Sure,' the Yank agreed. 'It would have been curtains for us, and them backroom boys in Washington would have had to do without their water. And another thing, you know who squealed on us?'

'What do you mean — squealed on us?' Crooke snapped.

'That little creep — Weed. I didn't trust the bastard, right from the start!'

They stared at him incredulously.

'Yeah — ex-cook he calls himself. Did you guys see how he handled that carbine? He was the only one here besides ourselves who knew what the mission was. And where is the little rat now? Supposed to be in the bog with the shits — that's where!'

The Destroyers acted as one. They doubled round the house to where the latrine stood, surrounded by a square of khaki-coloured sacking. They burst in to find a fat clerk ruminating in one of the wooden cubicles, an old copy of the *Stars and Stripes* in his pudgy hands.

'Did you see that little bastard — Weed?' the Yank snapped.

'You mean the feller who came in with you last night?'

'Yeah.'

'He was round the back when I came in five minutes ago,' the clerk stuttered.

The Destroyers ran to the back. But they were too late. Weed had gone, only his glasses remained, resting neatly on the scrubbed white-wood seat.

And then the awful realization overcame Crooke. He clapped his hand to his blouse. The bottle had gone and the only person who could have taken it was Weed.

TWO: THE TRAP

'There are many people in important positions in London who would be only too glad if Eisenhower were removed from his position. They'd propose Monty as his replacement like a shot. And you know what that would mean — a complete breakdown of Allied unity.'
Commander Mallory to the Destroyers, 19 December 1944

CHAPTER 13

The big, red-faced American Colonel with the golden sphinx of the US Counter Intelligence Corps on his lapel looked across at Commander Mallory, in mute enquiry. Mallory, his face pale and his nerves still tense from that nightmare ride out of St Vith during which a German bullet had put an end to Abel's life quicker than the effects of radiation which had slowly been eating away his body, nodded. 'All right, gentlemen, I'm going to give you it straight.' He stared at the Destroyers seated opposite him in the big Brussels HQ. 'You present me with a problem — one helluva problem. And this is no time for difficult problems. The situation is distinctly dicey.'

The Colonel, who looked as if he enjoyed his whisky and his women, allowed himself a fleeting smile, but his eyes did not light up. Colonel Dawson was a very tough individual. 'I don't think I need tell you that both the First and Ninth US Armies have been pretty badly hit and it's having an effect behind the line, believe you me.' He waved a big paw at the tall French window. 'Out there in the capital, there are twenty thousand American soldiers on the run. Imagine what that means — a whole division of GI's who've gone over the hill, living on their wits now with every man's hand against them. Add to that thousands of Belgian civilians running the black market and the refugees pouring into town by the hour because they think this is going to be 1940 all over again. Add that all together, gentlemen, and you've got a pretty damn tricky situation.'

The Destroyers nodded their understanding. On their way back from Ross's battalion they had seen the hopeless confusion caused by the sudden German offensive. Everywhere the roads were littered with the debris of a retreating army: guns, tanks, trucks scattered along the narrow, cobbled highways; in every town and village they had passed through, they had noted the sullen, silent looks of the civilians, the absence of national flags and pictures of the Belgian royal family which had decorated every window on the way up to St Vith. This was the 'big bugout', as the GI's called it.

Crooke cleared his throat and looked across at Mallory, who was fitting a cigarette into his ivory holder with trembling fingers. For a while, he knew, he would have to take over; the Commander was still too shaken. 'I appreciate we're asking you a lot, Colonel. I know how difficult things are at the moment. But we've got to find Weed. It is absolutely vital that he's found!'

'I'm well aware of that, Lieutenant Crooke. I can assure you I've had several assorted generals beating my ear on the phone all morning about that particular subject. All I want to make clear to you is the complexity of the job.' He rose and walked to the window. It was snowing. The sky was a leaden grey.

'That town out there, gentlemen,' he said, 'is wide open. No one back in the States could imagine what's going on there at this moment. Every possible crime — every possible vice. It's in the air. The Belgians think it's forty all over again. The Germans are coming back — this is going to be our last Christmas. Let's live it up — have one last desperate fling — before the whole damn shoot goes bust.' His voice rose angrily. 'Hell, in one stockade alone here, we've got one hundred and eighty officers on black market charges! One guy even tried to hijack a trainload of cigarettes for the guys up front, and not one of the bastards had less than five thousand dollars on him when he was picked up. Imagine that — *one hundred and eighty of them!*

'Colonel,' Crooke said softly.

Colonel Dawson nodded. 'Okay, okay, I know I'm running off at the mouth. But it's a bad time — a helluva bad time.' He walked back to the desk and, picking up a pair of steel-rimmed GI glasses, stared down at the papers on his desk. 'But we *have* gotten something on your man since last night. He hitched a ride on a ration truck leaving the 2nd Battalion and got as far as the regimental HQ. Then he disappeared. He must be a smart little bastard. But we think we picked him up again at zero five hours this morning at Dinant on the River Meuse.'

He referred to the paper. 'A jeep was reported missing there — from outside an MP barracks incidentally. The corporal in charge of it forgot to carry out the usual immobilization drill. Said he thought it would be safe outside an MP HQ. As if anything is safe these days. From there it's my guess he headed for Brussels here. They all come here first. It's a big town with plenty of easy broads — a deserter doesn't last long with no papers, without a woman whose room'll serve as a good base for black market operations. And Brussels is full of women looking for a good time — booze, smokes, silk stockings, jitterbugging.'

'But how do you know that the man who stole the jeep is Weed?' Mallory asked.

'How?' Dawson echoed the question. 'Because the German agent who's gonna be shot in exactly —' he consulted his watch — 'one hour said that Doctor Deschner was to report here for his mission.'

'And who is Doctor Deschner, Colonel?' Crooke asked.

'Weed, we think.' Colonel Dawson picked up his cap. 'Come on, let's go and see the German. He can give you the real poop.'

The big Chevrolet staff car nosed its way through the centre of Brussels. The streets were crowded with troops from half-a-dozen different Allied armies: Scots in kilts with red knees, shivering Indian supply troops in turbans, squat Polish tankmen with heavy, stiff epaulettes, GI's wearing captured German leather jackets and the thick grey felt boots the enemy wore in Russia. But it was the women who caught the Destroyers' attention. Stockingless, perched on high wooden-heeled shoes and huddled in rabbit-skin jackets, they offered their skinny war-worn bodies to the greedy hands of the soldiers, descending in their hundreds from the muddy leave trucks, seizing this last chance of quick, fleeting pleasure.

Finally the staff car cleared the centre of town and picked up speed for a while until they came in sight of the US stockade: a low, grim building, heavy with that same prison smell of sweat, stale food and fear which the Destroyers knew so well.

Four frozen-faced MPs, armed with tommy guns, stopped them at the big, iron-barred gate. 'You'd think anybody was eager to get into the bloody place,' Stevens said scornfully, as they scrutinized the Colonel's documents.

Dawson grinned. 'Max security,' he explained, as they drove through. 'This is the stockade where we keep the big wheels.' The heavy gates clanged behind them. Inside a couple of bent-shouldered men in ragged battledress with 'PW' stencilled in white on their jackets were sweeping away the slush under the supervision of an MP, armed with a sawn-off shotgun.

They got out of the car and sloshed through the mess into the main building where they were met by a tall MP captain in an immaculate uniform, the West Point class ring gleaming on his finger. He saluted rigidly.

Dawson acknowledged his salute casually. 'Is Krause able to talk?'

'Yessir, the doc gave him a shot,' the captain snapped, looking straight ahead unwaveringly, as if he were studying some spot far behind the colonel's right shoulder.

'Okay, let's go and see him.'

'First time I've ever been in the nick, sir, and managed to get out again on the same day,' Stevens whispered to Commander Mallory.

Mallory contented himself with a curt nod. His mind was still full of that moment of terror when the SS had come slinking out of the trees, before the firing had broken into his sleep — and then Major Abel hopping on one leg through the snow, desperately trying to escape from the trap, until the tracer had ripped open his back.

The party climbed a series of stone stairs and halted in front of two MPs sitting on rickety wooden stools before a metal door. The two MPs jumped to their feet when they saw the brass.

'Open the door,' Dawson ordered.

The taller of the two placed his grease gun on the stool and opened the door. The Colonel strode in, followed by the Destroyers. The little cell was bare save for a chair, a crucifix on the wall and a white cot in the corner. But the cell's occupant was not sitting on the cot. He was standing at the window, gazing out at the snowy courtyard.

'Krause,' Dawson said softly.

Slowly the German prisoner turned round. He was a tall, big-boned man with long arms and large red hands that hung down below the sleeves of his dyed, American fatigues. The clothes were much too small for his frame and made him seem all the more pathetic.

'Sure they're treating you okay, Krause?' Dawson asked.

The man nodded slowly. 'Yes, thank you, Colonel.'

'Krause,' Dawson asked softly, 'I'd like to ask you again what your mission was when we captured you at Huy? Dressed in American uniform. That's why —' he added for the Destroyers' benefit, but didn't finish his sentence.

'I belonged to the Stielau Unit,' Krause said in a faraway voice. 'There were eighty of us. Our task was to penetrate the American front on the first day of the offensive, commit acts of sabotage and reconnoitre the crossings of the River Meuse for our tanks.' He said the words as if he were repeating a lesson he had learned a long time ago, but for what reason he no longer knew.

'And what exactly was this Stielau outfit?' Dawson prompted.

'It belonged to the tank brigade commanded by *Obersturmbannführer* Otto Skorzeny,' he replied, his voice void of any emotion.

The Destroyers exchanged glances. Dawson saw their reaction. 'Have you heard of him?' he asked.

Crooke smiled. 'Oh yes, we've heard of him all right, Colonel. We were in Italy last year when he snatched Mussolini from his prison on the Gran Sasso with his paratroopers.'

'Okay, so you know that he's a real tough baby, a guy who'll stop at nothing to carry out his Führer's orders. In our book, Skorzeny is one of the most dangerous men in Western Europe today.'

'But Colonel,' Crooke said, 'what has this got to do with us and Weed? And who is this Doctor Deschner you've mentioned?'

The name had its effect. The German who was soon to be shot looked at Crooke. 'Deschner — or Weed as you call him — is *Obersturmbannführer* Skorzeny's key agent — the filthy swine! And the man who betrayed me and my companions.'

The Destroyers looked at Colonel Dawson for enlightenment.

'Ten days before the offensive started, one of our agents in the Eifel was given the dope that German commando troops in US uniform would try to cross the bridge at Huy. He wasn't told why, but we had the bridge staked out when Captain Krause and his men tried to cross it in their jeep. That's why he's here this morning. But this is the important point. The description our agent in the Eifel gave of the German who tipped him off tallies with that of Weed — or to give him his real name, Doctor Ignaaz Deschner, one of the specialists Skorzeny borrowed from the *Abwehr*.'

Suddenly the Destroyers understood why the blond German dressed in GI uniform had called out his curious question about the doctor. 'But why should Weed betray his own comrades?' Stevens asked. 'It don't stand to reason, sir.'

The condemned man answered for Dawson. 'Because our capture in American uniform forty-eight hours ago has led to a massive search for saboteurs behind your lines. Confusion everywhere, with thousands of your troops looking for spies behind every bush. For a calculating swine like Deschner it was worth sacrificing me and my comrades for the sake of...' He broke off and his lips began to tremble violently.

Heavy boots were marching down the long corridor. The men in the cell stood silent like characters at the end of a third-rate play, frozen in their melodramatic postures.

There was a jangle of heavy keys and the door creaked open. The prison chaplain — a full colonel, helmeted and wearing a trench coat, but with a black satin stole around his neck — was standing there. In his hands he held a small black book.

The Destroyers stepped back and dropped their gaze. The chaplain began to read from the black book in a soft, rapid voice. The condemned man listened in blank incomprehension. Finally the chaplain stopped and turned his head as if he were ashamed to look the German in the face.

The tall MP captain snapped an order. Two MPs pushed past the Destroyers and took the German by the arms.

'Weed's mission?' Crooke hissed, as they led him out.

Dawson did not seem to hear. His eyes were fixed on the spectacle which was taking place in front of him. As the two MPs marched their prisoner out of the door, he followed. They led Krause and his two shivering companions across the frozen ground, which had been cleared of snow, to the three posts, newly painted black.

A soldier stepped out from behind the platoon of MPs, who were going to carry out the executions. He carried a pot of paint. Carefully he painted a blue stripe on the left leg of each prisoner's fatigues. The Destroyers knew why; technically the Germans would not now be shot in US uniform. Then two soldiers had tied the three Germans to the posts, wrapping bright yellow ropes round their chests and ankles and tied their arms behind the posts. That finished, the MP captain pulled three black cloths from his pocket. He moved smartly from prisoner to prisoner, as if he were carrying out some sort of military drill, offering them the black bands for their eyes. They all refused. He shrugged slightly and nodded to the two soldiers. They pinned large white paper circles over the prisoners' hearts. The Germans followed the movements of their hands almost curiously.

Finally the prisoners were ready. The MP officer marched back to the waiting squad. He rapped out an order. The first row of twelve men dropped to one knee. Another order. The rifles went up. The MP captain barked a final order. The rifles rang out. In the trees beyond the field the rooks rose, cawing hoarsely.

As the sound of the rifle fire echoed and died away, Colonel Dawson turned to the Destroyers. 'Brave men,' he said softly, 'brave, foolish men.' His voice hardened again. 'You asked me what Weed's mission is?'

'Yes.'

'That man out there.' They knew he meant Krause. 'He told me that Weed's mission was to assassinate someone.'

'And who was that someone?' Mallory asked.

'The Supreme Commander, General Eisenhower.'

CHAPTER 14

The night's sleep had worked wonders. Commander Mallory was still pale, but the thin fingers which held the inevitable cigarette no longer trembled and the faraway frozen look had gone from his eyes. 'Morning,' he snapped without ceremony as they filed into the office Dawson had put at his disposal. 'Sit down and let's get down to business.'

Stevens nudged Muhammed. 'The old man's back in form,' he whispered.

'Yes, and you and your Egyptian companion will be back in Catterick Military Prison, Stevens, if you don't keep your hands off those American cigarettes! Colonel Dawson told me this morning that there had been a remarkable outbreak of petty thieving in the last twenty-four hours here.' Mallory stared at the little Cockney severely, but there was a twinkle in his eyes. 'He attributes the thefts to the black market. I have other ideas.'

Stevens looked down at his stubby fingers. 'You wouldn't begrudge the ordinary squaddie the odd spit-and-a-draw, would you, sir?'

Mallory dismissed the subject. 'All right, then, as I see the situation, it goes like this. Some time or other during 15 December, the Germans must have come across Klaus Schurz waiting at the chapel in the woods. They killed him and...'

'You mean that little bastard Weed killed him and staked him out for us!' the Yank interrupted.

'Possibly it was Weed. We don't know. What we do know is that he tumbled to the fact that Schurz wasn't in those woods by chance. He was there to make contact with someone from the Allied side.'

'And he used us to get him through our lines,' Crooke said. 'Very cunning indeed. No questions asked — nothing. He was just another stray — and we had sufficient authority to get him through any checkpoint without any trouble whatsoever.'

'But he fired on his own people,' Peters protested.

Mallory lit another cigarette. 'A thing like that wouldn't worry Weed. You heard what Krause said of him yesterday. Obviously our little man is quite ruthless. Besides, his mission is worth a couple of divisions of ordinary footsloggers. Remember, there are many people in important positions in London who would be only too glad if Eisenhower were removed from his position. They'd have Monty as his replacement like a shot. And you know what that would mean — a complete breakdown of Allied unity, with Washington and London slanging each other like fishwives. In the middle of this new offensive, we can't afford a crisis of that kind.'

'Yes, I know all that,' Crooke said, 'but we all seem to have forgotten one thing — the sample of water. What are we going to do about that? Isn't that our first priority?'

Mallory breathed out a thin, blue stream of smoke. 'Our first priority, Crooke, is to catch Weed. We must prevent any attempt on General Eisenhower's life and at the same time we've got to get that bottle back. Philby telephoned me before breakfast. "C" is screaming out for action.'

'Good,' Crooke said. 'But where do we look for him? Colonel Dawson has already told us that to look for him here in Brussels is like looking for a needle in a haystack. There are thousands of men on the run living here.'

Mallory gave him a knowing smile. 'I know — virtually impossible. But there is one way to lure him out of his hiding place.'

'And that is?'

'Well, wherever General Eisenhower is, we'll undoubtedly find Weed, won't we?'

'But you can't do that!' Crooke protested. 'You can't use the Supreme Commander to bait a trap.'

'Too late,' Mallory said calmly. 'General Eisenhower is already here. In fact,' he rose casually and stubbed out his cigarette, 'you're going to meet him — now.'

General Dwight D. Eisenhower was sitting behind Dawson's big desk when they marched in. He was exactly as they remembered him from Algiers the year before — high, balding forehead, wide mouth, bright eyes. But the broad grin of the summer of 1943 was gone and there was a worried look on his face. Obviously he was troubled by the extent of the German attack at a time when everyone at SHAEF had been confidently predicting that the war would be over by Christmas.

'General,' said Dawson, standing attentively at his side, 'these are the Destroyers I have been telling you about.'

Eisenhower mustered each one of the men standing rigidly to attention in front of him in the high room. 'At ease, soldiers,' he said. 'So you're the fellers who have been having all the adventures?'

Crooke looked at the General curiously. Eisenhower had apparently forgotten that he had met them in Algiers before they had set off on the Italian mission. He dismissed the thought next instant. He had to warn the General. He couldn't allow Dawson and Mallory to risk his life like this. He cleared his throat loudly.

Eisenhower looked up at his pale, tense face. 'What's on your mind, Lieutenant?'

'Sir,' Crooke began hesitantly, 'you must forgive me, but you can't take a chance like this. I must beg you to return to Paris where you're safe. You can't risk this man attempting to kill you!'

For a moment there was a shocked silence. Dawson, Mallory and the General stared at him, as if he had just dropped his pants in front of them.

Then Dawson laughed out loud. His big hand came down and clapped the Supreme Commander familiarly on the shoulder. 'Hot dog,' he cried enthusiastically. '*It worked, Joe!*'

While the Destroyers stared at the brass aghast, the General swung his feet on the table, scratched a match alight on the sole of his shoe and lit a big cigar, his body shaking with stifled laughter.

'Well for God's sake relax!' Dawson exclaimed, 'you're not seeing things, believe me!'

But the Destroyers could not take their eyes off the Supreme Commander as he sprawled there in his chair, a cigar in his mouth, grinning at them.

'All right,' Mallory said, 'tell them before they burst a blood vessel.'

'Okay, fellers. The fact is the idle slob now sprawled in my chair is not General Eisenhower. The Commander-in-Chief is still safely back in Versailles, sitting in the middle of a battalion of MPs assigned to the HQ to guard him — and undoubtedly blowing his top at being confined to his quarters till the assassination scare blows over.'

'But who's this?' Crooke breathed.

'Joe Stead of the Army Air Corps, who last month took a pretty nice jump in rank — from corporal to five star general to be exact.'

The man on the chair waved a lazy hand at them. 'Glad to meet you all.'

'You see,' Colonel Dawson continued, 'all our major leaders have doubles these days. Your Monty has, as well as Mr Churchill. It's an ideal way of throwing the enemy off the scent of anything important. General so-and-so is in Africa. In fact the real general is in London planning something else. In short, the double business pays good dividends. Hence we've given General Ike two doubles. You are now looking at one. Joe,' he added, 'was once an actor.'

'Not a very good one,' Stead said easily. 'I've found a home in the Army. Here I eat regularly at least.'

'Very goddamn neat, Colonel,' the Yank said, 'but what the hell's he here for?'

'To pay an official visit to the Belgian capital tomorrow afternoon. Understandably morale is pretty low here at the moment. The General's visit will be a shot in the arm for the civilians.'

'It's our belief,' Mallory took up the explanation, 'that Weed will make an attempt on the General's life while he's here — the news has been *leaked* to the Belgian papers. He'll hear it for sure and if he makes the attempt, we'll nab him.'

'You'd goddamn well better — before he gets me!' Stead protested.

'Don't worry,' Mallory reassured him. 'We'll save you for your public.'

'What public?'

Dawson walked over to a big map of the centre of Brussels which decorated one wall. 'This is the way we've got it planned. The Supreme Commander will arrive by special train at 1400 hours. Here, at the Gare du Nord, where he'll be welcomed by high-ranking Allied military personnel. That should take about fourteen to eighteen minutes. From there he will ride down several of the main boulevards to show himself to the locals.' He traced the route with his finger. 'Until he arrives here at the old Hotel de Ville, where he will be given a civic reception.'

Stead groaned. 'Not another civic reception! The General's gonna get angry if I get too fat. I'll have to go on a diet again — just before Christmas too. You see,' he explained to the Destroyers, 'I've got to keep the same figure as General Eisenhower — and he doesn't eat too much. It's murder trying to keep my weight down. But as the boss says — you've got to shape up or ship out, and brother, it's too damn cold up in the line at this time of the year.'

Mallory took over again. 'Now then, where do you think that friend Weed might have a crack at the General?'

Peters spoke first. 'There are three possibilities — the station, the drive, the civic reception. I'd guess the drive, sir.'

Mallory agreed. 'The streets are a danger. There are a lot of people to watch and control. Anything could happen.'

'Let's call the whole thing off,' Stead said in mock alarm. 'I'll take my chance up the line. Perhaps I can get a job as a cook or something.'

'Don't worry, Joe,' Dawson said. 'We'll take good care of you. You're too precious to be bumped off — *yet*.'

Mallory continued. 'The streets sound all right, but it's well known that the General has been travelling around in an armoured vehicle since the offensive started and we can't change the pattern of his habits now. Weed might get suspicious. Besides the Belgian troops lining the route will be facing in towards the crowd. Apparently that's always the way on the continent.'

'So it's the shindig, sir,' Stevens suggested.

'Yes, that's our guess. The General will be seated in one spot for at least two hours. There'll be flunkies and waiters coming and going all the time and a crowd of civvie guests, who've been invited at such short notice that we can't vet them all. If Weed has a go anywhere tomorrow, it'll be at that reception.'

CHAPTER 15

Seven abreast the band of the Brigade of Guards packed the shabby Belgian street as they swung up to the station. At their head the massive drum major, resplendent in red and silver, swung his mace with majestic ease, his eyes fixed on some far horizon, blind to the miserable world of the half-starved civilians packed in on both sides. But their stirring music had little effect. It was snowing hard and the flakes falling on the crowd seemed to deaden their mood even more, as they waited outside the Gare du Nord for the Allied Supreme Commander to arrive.

To Crooke there was something ominous about the crowd's silence. Perched on a lamppost, the Destroyers' CO looked around to check that his men were still in place — Muhammed and Stevens to the left of the station exit, the Yank and Peters to the right, Thaelmann between Dawson and Mallory in the second row of the welcoming party. Nothing distinguished them from the other Allied soldiers doing a little sightseeing, save that their eyes moved around a lot and their hands were kept tightly clasped on the pistols in their pockets.

The band came to a halt. The drum major rapped out a series of commands. Heavy boots crashed down hard on the slush. They turned and faced the exit. The General should be coming out at any moment.

Crooke ran his eye along the line of tall buildings which faced the station. Most of them were poorly disguised brothels, catering for the needs of Allied soldiers, with here and there a legitimate hotel. All of them were regular rabbit warrens, which offered ideal hiding places for any sniper, but there was little

Dawson and his men had been able to do about it; even now scores of Allied soldiers on leave, haversacks slung over their shoulders, were waiting patiently to enjoy the services of the 'girls'. Dawson simply did not have enough men to screen the brothels and to guard the Hotel de Ville.

The minutes passed. The snow kept falling. Soldiers came out of the houses to be greeted by jeers from the waiting crowd before crossing the street to the green-light prophylactic station to undergo the compulsory anti-VD treatment. Outside the station the Belgians shuffled their feet in the cold.

Suddenly an American staff officer came hurrying out of the station. The drum major raised his mace. The band broke into 'The Stars and Stripes For Ever'. On both sides of the exit the twin lines of white-helmeted American MPs snapped to attention. In front of Dawson a bemedalled white-haired Belgian general, in a uniform that was much too big for him, ushered a little girl in knee socks forward. Her legs were pink with cold and the big bunch of roses in her hand trembled as she shivered. The MPs saluted. The music grew louder. A group of staff officers in immaculate olive drab jackets and perfectly creased 'pinks' fanned out on both sides of the exit. A second later, General Dwight D. Eisenhower, Supreme Commander of all Allied Forces in Western Europe, made his appearance. He paused at the exit and beamed to left and right, with that wide-grinned smile known to cinema audiences throughout the western hemisphere.

In the continental fashion the crowd began to applaud. The white-haired Belgian general gave the little girl a push. She stumbled forward. As Eisenhower bent down to kiss the little girl presenting him the flowers, Crooke caught a glimpse of Stevens over his shoulder. He was smiling proudly, his thumb raised in triumph, as if he were stage-managing the whole deception and everything were going well. The crowd's applause grew a little louder. The little girl was shoved aside by the old general. Eisenhower began to shake hands, pausing here and there along the line of worthies to exchange a few words with those who could speak English. The Guards band played on lustily. A Cadillac forced its way slowly through the crowd, a stiff, red flag with five brass stars decorating its bonnet. It hit a bump in the road and Crooke could see how it sank on its springs. Obviously it was armoured.

Dawson, standing next to Eisenhower, whispered something to the latter. He quickened his pace. A tight line of MPs on motorcycles formed a V in front of the Cadillac. The driver sprang out of the car and opened the door. The band redoubled its efforts. This was their last chance. The Supreme Commander nodded graciously to the drum major. Crooke took his hand off his pistol. Eisenhower was nearly in the car. He'd better start thinking of the problems in the Hotel de Ville.

Then it happened. Eisenhower had put his right foot in the car. The crowd had stopped clapping. Here and there civilians at the back began to drift away. The show was almost over, when suddenly there was the sharp crack of a rifle, followed by a high-pitched scream. The drum major clutched his eye with one hand. The mace clattered to the snowy ground. Slowly his knees started to buckle beneath him. For one moment there was an awful silence. No one moved. Eisenhower stood with his right foot poised in mid air, Dawson at his side, open-mouthed with shock.

Then all hell broke loose. Women screamed. The group of high-ranking Allied officers scattered hastily in case more shots were to follow. The little girl who had presented the bouquet disappeared under their feet. The guardsmen broke ranks and crouched around the dying drum major. MPs blew their whistles and pushed through the dense crowd.

'*La bas, la bas!*' the crowd screamed. 'He'll fire again,' someone yelled in English. The crowd scattered, fighting to get out of the line of fire.

Crooke dropped from the lamppost. Behind him the Yank and Peters were fighting their way through the terrified press, revolvers drawn. As he ran, he thought of the newsreel he'd seen of De Gaulle's entry into Paris that summer and the panic when the snipers had opened fire from the rooftops; hundreds of people had been crushed to death. Would their plan to catch Weed result in a similar tragedy?

He had not reckoned with Corporal Stead. He acted his role of Supreme Commander to perfection. Pushing Dawson, who had placed his own big body in front of the ex-actor, as if to protect him, aside he stretched up to his full height and raised his clasped hands above his head in the old prizefighter's gesture of victory.

Its effect was instantaneous. The panic was stopped. The civilians rose. People began to clap. First here and there. Then more and more. The applause grew. It became a cheer. A great roar of approval rose from the crowd. Stead got into the Cadillac. Swiftly the driver rammed home the gear. The car drew away from the kerb, surrounded by its escort of motorcycle police. The danger was over!

As the crowd calmed down, the Destroyers pushed their way across to the row of grey stone buildings from which the shot had come. 'Muhammed and Stevens,' Crooke ordered, 'you stay here and watch the roofs.' He turned to the others who were pushing through the crowd of puzzled soldiers waiting still to enter the brothels. 'Thaelmann, you come with me.

We'll take the roof. Yank and Peters, work your way up from the bottom.'

Like the well-trained team they were, the Destroyers spread out to execute his orders, while Thaelmann and Crooke raced up the rickety stairs of the nearest building.

Panting for breath, Crooke saw what he was looking for in the gloomy attic — the skylight. 'Grab that ladder over there!' he gasped, 'and give me a hand.'

Thaelmann picked up the ladder lying in the shadows and together they placed it below the skylight. Crooke clambered up and forced the window. An icy wind hit him in the face. Through the flurries of snow he could see that the roof was angled at forty-five degrees, with patches of slippery grey slate showing through the white cover of snow. 'Thaelmann,' he called down, 'I'm going to check…'

There was a sharp crack as a slug whistled through the snow. Slate splinters flew up a yard away. He reeled back, hanging on to the ladder with one hand, flecks of blood starting from his face where he had been struck by the slate.

'Have you been hit, sir?' Thaelmann cried.

'It's nothing. The bastard's up there. I'm going up to get him.'

Sticking the pistol in his belt, Crooke levered himself up and out with both hands. Narrowing his eyes against the wind, he stared at the big chimney ahead. If Weed were hiding anywhere, it would be there. But how the devil, he asked himself, had he managed to fire at Stead from this direction? The building was set at a forty-five degree angle from the station!

The next instant he had his answer. A strange blue-steel object wormed its way round the edge of the chimney. He ducked — just in time. Again there was a crack and a slug struck the snow a few feet away. Crooke fired. Brick dust spurted up from the edge of the chimney. 'Weed,' he bellowed against the howl of the wind. 'Give up! You haven't got a chance. The place is surrounded!'

His only answer was a bullet.

Crooke reached out his free hand and sought for a handhold below the cover of snow. He found one and worked his way forward, trying to get some purchase on the guttering with his toes. But it was blocked and smooth with frozen snow.

Weed fired again. Crooke flattened himself as best he could against the roof, feeling his fingers already beginning to grow numb with the biting cold, and the slug whistled by harmlessly. Now he knew how Weed had done it. The strange blue-steel object was the muzzle of a rifle; but a rifle the like of which Crooke had never seen in his life before. Its barrel was bent at an angle *so that it could fire round corners!*

But Crooke had no time to ponder on his discovery. Suddenly he was sliding feet first, face down, his fingers scrabbling madly for a handhold. Down below, the crowds of civilians watching the drama on the roof gasped with horror.

Crooke felt his feet slide over the guttering. The strangled cry of fear died on his lips. His hands caught hold of something. Whatever it was ripped off his thumbnail. A wave of agonizing pain shot up his arm, but he held on. He grabbed one of the hooks firemen used to anchor their ladders.

Forcing himself to be calm, he flexed the muscles of his arms. Slowly — terribly slowly — he began to haul himself upwards. Inch by inch, the blood pouring down the back of one of his hands, the wind whipping the snow into his face, he pulled his legs over the edge. Then he was lying there face down in the snow, his heart pounding like a sledgehammer, all his strength gone.

An age passed, so it seemed. The wind howled and the snow beat down on his inert body. How long he lay there, Crooke did not know. It could have been only seconds. When he looked up again at the brick chimney, the would-be killer and his strange weapon had gone, and Thaelmann was shouting from the skylight. 'He's down here, sir! Barricaded himself into a room in the attic!'

Moments later Thaelmann was helping him in through the skylight, his eyes mirroring his shock at Crooke's appearance: the torn uniform, the bleeding frost-whitened hands and the snow-covered face. Gently Thaelmann lowered his CO to the floor. 'It's all right, sir,' he said. 'He can't get away. We've got him trapped down there.'

He pointed down the length of the attic. There was a little walled-off space at the far end, where the Yank and Peters were crouched, pistols at the ready.

Groggily Crooke staggered towards them, pistol held in a bleeding hand which trembled violently. 'Weed,' he cried, as the other Destroyers prepared to rush the door, 'come on out. You've had it!'

A hole suddenly appeared in the door. They ducked as the bullet ricocheted off the bare brick wall of the attic.

'All right, you little bastard!' the Yank roared, 'I'm gonna count to three and then I'm coming in! If you aren't out by then, *I swear I'll cut your goddamn nuts off!*'

'ONE!'

From inside the little attic room came the sound of mumbled cursing and fumbling, as if Weed were attempting to reload his strange weapon.

'TWO.' The Yank clicked back the hammer of his big colt.

'THREE!'

There was a strange click. Then with a great crash the door flew off its hinges. Hastily the Destroyers ducked as the acrid cloud of grenade smoke streamed outwards, carrying the splintered wreck of a door with it.

Coughing and spluttering, they rushed in, pistols at the ready. But the sniper was already dead.

His body lay arched on the remnants of an ancient chaise longue. A rough mat of scorched hair rose up straight from his blackened face. The thin grey smoke rose from the gory mess of his chest to which he had clutched the grenade. Now that hand had gone. All that was left was a red, dripping stump. The would-be killer's good hand flopped out over the edge of the couch, dripping blood.

Thaelmann broke the silence. 'It's not Weed,' he said tonelessly.

'How do you know?'

'His thumb — look at his thumb.'

Holding his nose against the smell of burned, charred flesh, the Yank bent over the shattered corpse and carefully examined the strange mark tattooed between the thumb and forefinger of the dead man's hand. 'It looks like a V,' he said slowly, straightening up again, 'like an orange V.' Then he nodded. 'You're right, Thaelmann, Weed didn't have anything like that on his hand when we saw him last.'

Crooke, swaying still after so narrowly escaping death on the roof, stared numbly at the little tattoo. An orange V! Where had he heard about that mark? But his brain refused to function. All he could think of was that Weed had escaped; the little *Abwehr* agent was still at large with the priceless secret in his possession.

CHAPTER 16

'You know, over these last years the papers and the films have made us think that, apart from a handful of quislings — the people of Occupied Europe hated Hitler,' Mallory said, gazing around the little circle of soldiers in Colonel Dawson's office. 'But that was not always the case. The Nazis were welcomed enthusiastically by some minorities in most of the countries they took over in the first years of the war. Today the German Army is full of men of non-German nationality; French, Belgians, Norwegians, Danes — the lot, all of whom volunteered to fight for the German cause. But no people in Occupied Europe co-operated as much as the Belgian Flemings. As perhaps you know, this country is dominated by the French-speaking Walloons. They run the government, the economy, the administration and the army. The Walloons run the country and the Flemings, who make up half the population, have always felt out of things — rather like a lot of country bumpkins, speaking an impossible dialect, Flemish, who are only good enough to carry out the rough work for the French-speaking bosses. Naturally the Germans were not slow to make use of this hatred of the Flemings for the Walloons. Back in the Great War they tried to convince the Flemings that they were members of the Greater German Community. And of course, as soon as the Nazis came along with their crackpot racial theories, the Flemings were classed as Aryans and racial brothers. So when the Germans took over Belgium in 1940, the Flemings flocked to their standards by the thousand. At this moment there is a whole Belgian SS Division fighting in the East against the Russians. In August and September, when our troops moved into Belgium, the whole Flemish dream came apart. The great majority of them resigned themselves to the fact that the Walloons would take over again, but there were a few who were not content to accept the new situation just like that — and they were naturally aided by the Germans who saw them as an ideal source of espionage behind our lines.'

'The *Broederbond*?' Colonel Dawson said.

'Yes, Colonel, the "Band of Brothers", a group of fanatical Flemings,' he added for the Destroyers' benefit, 'who still believe in Germany's victory and are prepared to do anything for the Germans.'

'This is all very interesting,' Crooke interposed, 'but I can't see what it's got to do with Weed and the chap who tried to kill Stead.'

'I'm coming to that. We know that Skorzeny's organization left behind some "sleepers" — German-trained agents — with the *Broederbond* when the Germans pulled out of Belgium in September. Two months ago our wireless experts informed the authorities that they were contacting Skorzeny's HQ at Friedensthal, just outside Berlin. We couldn't break their code, but the fact that they were in radio contact with Skorzeny indicates that the *Broederbond* was planned into this new German offensive. The events of this afternoon at the station prove, I think, that that is the case. You noted the orange V on the sniper's hand?'

The Destroyers nodded.

'It stands for "*Vlaams — Vrij — Voorwaarts*". Roughly "Flemish, free and forward!" That is the motto of the *Broederbond*.'

'And you think that Weed had contact with them, sir?'

'Not *had*, Stevens, but *has*. Obviously he is not a loner as we thought at first. His contacts here in Belgium were already established before he set off on his mission. And…'

'That's why the little bastard could afford to sell Krause up the river!' the Yank interrupted.

'Of course. Their capture and confession would cause confusion behind the Allied lines — an ideal set-up for Weed's own personal plan, for which he would get aid *not* from outside Belgium, but from *within*. Wherever Weed is at this moment, he must be laughing up his sleeve at us!'

'But fortunately we do know where he is,' Colonel Dawson said easily, 'or at least we think we do. You see, ever since we moved into Belgium in the fall, your intelligence folks and ourselves have been keeping an eye on the Flemish situation. Together with the commie resistance organization — sixty thousand strong and well armed with the weapons we dropped to them during the Occupation — they both present a potential danger to our lines of communication. Over these last two months or so the CIC has located the area of Flanders which contains the core of this pro-German Flemish resistance — the hangout of the *Broederbond*, if you like…' He turned to the map behind him. 'Here in the middle of the Flemish-speaking area between Brussels and Ghent — at the village of Fort op der Bergen. Apparently it has always been a kinda place of pilgrimage for the hard-core anti-Walloon Fleming. According to the legend when the Spaniards surrounded the place during the Middle Ages, the villagers held out there for fifty days. And then when they were down to eating rats and stewing bits of old leather to get some sort of nourishment, they slaughtered their kids rather than let them grow up under Spanish domination. Since the Flemish independence movement started in the late nineteenth century, Fort op der

Bergen has become a symbol of Flemish resistance to the foreigner, including, naturally, the French-speaking Walloon.'

'But Colonel, if you've known about this place being the headquarters of the *Broederbond* so long, why haven't you done anything about it before?' Crooke asked.

'There are a lot of reasons, Crooke, damn good reasons. Though I wish to hell now we'd have simply barrelled into Fort op der Bergen back in September with an armoured regiment and sorted the bastards out! But it's too late for that now. With this lousy surprise offensive on our hands, we can't afford to have a Belgian governmental crisis. And you can bet your bottom dollar that that's what would happen if we tried to smoke out the *Broederbond*. There'd be a helluva stink between the Flemings and Walloons — and we simply can't risk our lines of communication at this moment. Jesus, it's bad enough trying to keep the Germans boxed in the Ardennes!'

'So Weed is nicely tucked away in that Fort,' the Yank snorted in disgust. 'And we can't do a goddamn thing about it?'

Dawson sucked his teeth thoughtfully and looked at the door, as if he half expected to find someone listening there. 'Do nothing about it,' he echoed the Yank's words. 'Sure, Jones, we can't do anything about Fort op der Bergen officially. Officially, I repeat.' He paused and winked at the Destroyers with great solemnity. '*But unofficially —*'

CHAPTER 17

The big US Army truck rumbled along the dead-straight, cobbled Flemish road, fringed with naked poplars. In the back of the truck the six shabby German POWs in their ankle-length grey coats shivered with the icy cold, their unshaven faces peaked, the ends of their pinched noses red and dripping. Enviously they stared at their guard, a well-fed, young GI, wrapped in a fur parka, his hands clad in thick woollen gloves, Watchfully the soldier stared back at them. It was still quite a way to the Ghent POW cage and he wasn't about to lose them and end up with a rifle company in the line.

The truck started to slow down. They were approaching a crossroads with the usual checkpoint. The driver braked and the guard poked his head round the side of the canvas. A heavily-armed group of second-line troops stood there, aided by a tall, skinny Belgian policeman in a high cap and dark blue overcoat. The guard listened while they went through the usual rigmarole. 'What's the Bronx cheer? Who's Betty Grable's latest husband? Who's Goofy? What's the Dodgers?' The great German spy scare was having its effect. It seemed that half the US 1st Army was out checking the other half. Every darned crossroads since they had left Brussels at midday had had a checkpoint like this. Finally they were satisfied and waved the driver on. As they drove on, the Belgian policeman nodded imperceptibly at the German POWs, but the young guard did not notice the nod; he was too concerned with sticking another piece of gum into his mouth.

The kilometres passed. The Flemish countryside on both sides lay dead and empty under its heavy mantle of snow. The farmers were home, clustered around their big white-and-blue tiled stoves, reading their farming papers while their wives knitted or darned at their sides. In that white waste it seemed there was no one else alive save the guard and his miserable defeated German charges, the enthusiasm of that first tremendous day of the great offensive completely vanished now.

The truck roared into a village. It was nearly as empty as the countryside, save for a few sour-faced men in dark suits and wooden clogs standing at the door of the church. There was no smile on their faces when they caught sight of their 'liberators', just a kind of dogged peasant defiance. One of them took his clay pipe out of his mouth, hawked deeply and spat into the cobbled gutter.

'Happy little folk,' the GI said.

The German POWs did not react. They sat with hunched shoulders, resigned to their misery.

The driver was just regaining the main road at the far end of the village when a British motorcyclist roared into view. He stopped and held up his hand. A column of battered Churchill tanks clattered by, heading for the front. Suddenly a little pigtailed blonde girl with skinny legs and darned black stockings ran out of a doorway. She gave the men in the back of the truck the V-sign and threw in a loaf of local bread. It landed in the slushy mess on the truck's floor. Then she was gone, dashing into the doorway.

The guard cursed. Then, as the truck started again, he nodded to the nearest German, a wolfish looking man with half an ear missing. 'Okay, you can have the goddamn thing.' With the side of his combat boot he nudged it towards the German. 'Now pick it up nice and gentle.' He levelled his carbine. 'One false move, buddy, and I'll drill you.'

If the German did not understand the words, he understood the gesture well enough. Very carefully he bent down and picked up the bread, the greed sparkling in his eyes. He began to clean the loaf, using his sleeve to wipe off the wet dirt, while the rest of them stared at it in anticipation.

The truck rumbled on. It was beginning to get dark now and the temperature was sinking rapidly. The young GI looked at his watch. 'Another forty minutes,' he announced, 'and you guys'll be enjoying the home comforts of Ghent Cage.'

There was no answer from the Germans. Their eyes were still fixed on the loaf of bread. The German with half an ear was obviously puzzling how he could divide it equally between his comrades. Suddenly he looked across at the GI. '*Messer?*' he enquired and made a sawing motion with his hand across the loaf.

'Hell no!' the guard snapped. '*Nix Messer.* Do you think I want you guys to stick a knife in my ribs?'

The German must have understood. The look of greedy anticipation vanished from his face and he looked once more like a whipped dog.

The GI relented. 'Okay, no need to turn on the waterworks,' he said. 'Here gimme it; I'll cut it for you.'

The German's eyes lit up. He made the gesture of throwing the loaf to the American.

The GI nodded. 'Yeah, like that — nice and gentle, see.' He held out his free hand expectantly.

The German smiled his thanks, revealing large yellow teeth as he did so. He raised his hand. The GI waited. The German threw it — hard!

In the same instant that it hit the surprised GI in the face, another German, with silver SS runes at his collar, dived forward and caught the American by the knees. The GI's head shot back and hit the metal stanchion behind him. His helmet liner rolled to the floor. Hastily the SS man, who looked more like an Arab than an Aryan, grabbed him as he began to tilt forward. Almost gently he lowered the unconscious, bleeding American to the wet floor.

Swiftly the other POWs went into action. A sergeant with an empty hole where his eye should have been, grabbed the American's carbine and tossed it into a snowdrift at the side of the road. Two others bent down, ripped the GI's belt and tie off, and started to truss him up with them, while the rest sorted out their fur-backed packs at the end of the truck.

The sergeant stuck his head cautiously around the canvas, narrowing his one eye against the wind. The driver had not noticed anything. The German could see his face reflected in the driving mirror, as he crouched over his wheel. He turned back to the others and nodded. Swiftly they formed a little chain. The packs were passed rapidly from hand to hand, with the sergeant tossing them into the snow of the verges. He nodded to the SS man. Wordlessly he came to the edge of the truck, took a deep breath and then launched himself into space. He hit the road hard, rolled over expertly as if he had been trained for this kind of emergency, picked himself up quickly and darted into the ditch. One by one they all did the same. The sergeant took a last glance at the young GI trussed up on the floor. He lifted the man's head and slid the helmet liner under so that he could breathe more easily; then he, too, launched himself into space. Moments later the truck was rumbling on into the growing darkness, empty now save for the tied-up guard bouncing up and down on the wet floor.

Crooke kept guard while the rest of the Destroyers took the Sten machine pistol parts out of the German packs and clicked them together. 'Phase one went off pretty well,' he commented when they were finished.

'Yer,' Stevens said. 'I bet those Yanks are in for a surprise at Ghent POW camp!'

'Naturally,' Crooke replied, 'that's part of the plan. Colonel Dawson is going to ensure that the maximum fuss is made at that end when they discover that the birds have flown. They've got Flemish workers in the camp administration and Colonel Dawson is pretty sure they'll get the word back to the *Broederbond*.

'Hell,' the Yank said, 'I can't see why the hell we've got to go through all this crap to get at the bastards!'

'Well, apart from the political angle, which Commander Mallory explained to us, we wouldn't have stood a chance in hell of getting close to Fort op der Bergen if we'd have gone in in British uniform. You saw that Belgian policeman and the kid with the loaf of bread? It's obvious that all the villagers around here sympathize with the *Broederbond*. We wouldn't have got within sniffing distance before they would have been warned. This way, if anyone sees us, we're escaped German POWs on our way west, making for the German garrison bottled up in Dunkirk as likely as not. If they spot us, they'll look the other way and let us get on with it. Okay, let's move. I want to take them as soon as it gets dark.'

The Destroyers crouched in the ditch at the side of the steep rutted farm track which led into the village. Above them Fort op der Bergen sat on the top of the hill, black, squat and forbidding against the night sky. Nothing moved and no light showed. The fortress-like village seemed dead. But the soft lowing of cattle, the smell of animals and hay and the barking of a dog indicated that the place was inhabited.

'All right, here's the drill,' Crooke said. 'We'll tackle it this way. Off this track and up there over that field. Can you see where I mean?'

They nodded.

'That'll keep us under cover of the trees most of the way. The last ten yards or so between the trees and the first house we'll take at the double. Okay?'

'And what are we doing then?' Muhammed asked, rubbing his nose on the sleeve of his SS uniform, which bore the black and white armband of the SS Division *Hitlerjugend*.

'I'll tell you, Muhammed,' the Yank spoke before Crooke had a chance to answer. He pulled out his knife. 'I'm gonna give that little lecherous bastard Weed a going over with this.' He ran his thumb over its razor-sharp edge almost lovingly. Muhammed shivered.

Carefully they slipped into the trees and began to plough their way through the knee-deep snow up the hill. Every few moments, Crooke halted them and turning his head to the wind, listened. But there was no sound save for the lowing of the cattle.

Ten minutes later they reached the edge of the trees and crouched there panting, feeling the icy cold penetrate their soaked pants.

'Looks a big ten yards to me, sir,' Stevens said, staring intently at the first house. Crooke nodded, but said nothing. If the *Broederbond* was run on military lines and they had sentries posted, they'd be cut down before they had gone half the distance. 'Cover me,' he whispered. 'I'm taking off.'

'Let me…' Thaelmann began, but Crooke cut him short. 'I'm off,' he rapped. Crouched low, like a professional rugby player, expecting a machine gun to open up at any moment, Crooke pelted over the frozen snow. But there was no burst of fire — nothing.

Crooke vaulted over a low stone wall and flopped down in the garden of the first house, panting hard. He surveyed the house. Still no movement. Carefully he reached up and waved to the men crouched in the trees.

A few moments later they tried the door of the house. It was locked. But Stevens was prepared. He slipped his knife between the lock and the jamb of the door. He pressed hard and it swung open.

They were in a farm kitchen, smelling of hay, sour milk, manure and unwashed bodies. Curiously they looked around at the simple place, bare save for a scrubbed wooden table, four chairs, a metal stove for cooking and a crucifix on the wall, while Stevens and Muhammed went prowling into the next room. 'Looks as if the place is deserted, sir,' Peters said as Crooke peered through the curtain up the village street. It was empty too.

'Come and have a see at this, sir.' It was Stevens.

Crooke and the rest followed him into what was probably the 'best room', reserved for Sunday afternoon and celebrations. It was crammed full of highly-polished, overstuffed, leather furniture. The walls were covered in yellowing family photographs of plump women in black silk and awkward-looking men in high stiff collars. But Crooke had no time for the souvenirs of the past. He stared at the chest over which Muhammed was bent, his arms full of clothing. Underneath it lay six brand new rifles and a machine pistol, carefully wrapped in sacking.

Muhammed dropped the clothes and picked up the machine pistol. 'German, sir,' he said, 'Schmeisser.'

'Good work, Muhammed,' Crooke turned to the others, gathered in the flickering light of the candle which Thaelmann held. 'So Colonel Dawson wasn't wrong, eh? German rifles too. What would farmers be doing with them?'

'Typical agricultural reactionaries. Trying to turn the clock back,' Thaelmann said scornfully.

'Okay,' the Yank snapped, 'don't let's have no Communist sermons…'

He stopped short. There was the sound of clogs coming down the path to the house. Thaelmann blew out the candle while they arranged themselves on either side of the door. The sound of clogs stopped. There was the jingle of keys, a gasp of surprise and the door swung open.

Outlined against the dark sky outside, the Destroyers saw a tall, lean man, stooped a little under the weight of the churn he held in one hand. His mouth dropped open when he saw the Destroyers. But he didn't have time to recover.

'Get in,' Yank snapped and, grabbing the surprised Belgian civilian by his jacket, dragged him inside. Thaelmann kicked the door closed behind him and barked in German, 'Where is everybody? Is the German with them?'

In the light of the candle which Stevens had relit, Crooke could see the man's mouth clamp down stubbornly in refusal. But the Fleming did not know the Destroyers. Muhammed whipped out his wicked-looking knife. He did not take his eyes off the civilian, but asked Crooke out of the corner of his mouth, 'Shall I deal with him?'

The civilian licked his lips uneasily.

Muhammed made a sudden lunge at the man's lower body. He darted back in alarm. Muhammed pulled back just in time and laughed threateningly. 'Tell him, Thaelmann,' he said softly, his voice heavy with menace, 'if he is not speaking, I am going to hurt him. He will please no woman ever again.'

Thaelmann translated. Muhammed's eyes did not leave the civilian's face the whole time. The words had their effect. In crude but understandable German, the civilian gasped. 'They are all in the barn — at the end of the street. The Brotherhood is having a meeting.'

'And the German?'

'He is there, too.'

Crooke nodded to Peters who clubbed his fist and brought it down on the back of the Fleming's neck with all his strength. He slumped to the floor without a groan.

'String him up,' Crooke ordered.

Thaelmann and the Yank bent to carry out his order; he turned to Peters. 'You take care of the rear when we leave, Peters. If anybody comes looking for him, they'll be in for a surprise.'

Peters laughed softly and, slipping off his pack, undid the lacing. He delved inside and brought out what looked like animal droppings.

'If my old man was alive and saw that,' Stevens commented, 'he'd be out with his little spade collecting it for his tomatoes.'

CHAPTER 18

They were halfway down the cobbled street when they heard the well-remembered metallic strains. Crooke stopped and held up his hand. 'You heard it?'

Peters, behind him, whispered, 'Who's afraid of the Big Bad Wolf!'

'That's right. It came from up there.' Crooke pointed at the dark, squat shape of a barn in front of the ruins of the fort which gave the village its name. 'Come on, it's Weed all right.'

They slipped down the side of the little street. Once a door opened just in front of them. A blade of light cut into the gloom. There was a clatter of clogs, followed next moment by the splash of slops being thrown into the gutter. As the door closed again, Stevens said disgustedly, 'What a bloody pong! Don't them Belgians eat nothing but sodding, rotten cabbage!'

They crept on. The barn was a big place, half-timbered and wattle, with the faded yellow walls bulging outwards, as if they might collapse at any moment. From behind the door there came the soft chatter of voices, speaking in surprisingly subdued tones for farmers used to plenty of space and dumb animals which only seem to respond to loud noises and shouts.

Crooke climbed the four wooden steps which led to the thick oaken door. He bent and peered through a crack from which a beam of light escaped. He caught a glimpse of what looked like the bottom of a radio transmitter. Beyond it he could make out about twenty men standing in a group, their feet clad in manure-stained clogs or knee boots. He craned his neck, trying to see their faces. They were the usual broad, red farmers' faces. One face, however, stood out among them. It was pale, pudgy and cunning. Even without the steel-rimmed GI glasses which he had been wearing the last time Crooke had seen him, Weed was unmistakable.

With soft-footed caution, careful to avoid any noise on the rickety steps, he stole back down to the others and explained what he had seen. Then he gave out his orders. 'Thaelmann, you back me up. Yank, you cover both of us.'

'With pleasure,' the Texan said menacingly.

'I want him alive, remember, Yank,' Crooke said sternly. 'At least till I find out where the bottle is. Then he's yours.'

'Peters, you do your bit with the horse apples. Spread them across the road here. That should cut the barn off effectively from the rest of the place. Stevens and Muhammed — cover the back. As soon as we've sorted that lot out in there, we're coming out of the other end of the barn. You can give us covering fire, if we need it. Then we're down that hill and out of this place sharpish before we have the whole countryside up in arms against us. Got it?'

He looked round at their faces. Their features were tense, but there was no sign of fear in any of them. He felt proud of his men; the Destroyers would not let him down.

Crooke's free hand found the door handle and opened it. Surprisingly enough the ancient door did not squeak. Like a shadow he passed into the barn. Thaelmann and Yank followed, closing the door behind them noiselessly. They tensed there, Stens at the ready, surveying the little scene. The men were clustered around the transmitter, their backs to them, still unaware of their presence, their attention concentrated solely on the static chatter coming from the radio.

Crooke took a deep breath. 'Weed,' he said, surprised how normal his voice sounded. 'Turn round!' Weed spun round to stare at the three men standing in the shadows, backs to the wall. The farmers' faces showed no fear, just dumb amazement. Weed licked his lips. 'Lieutenant Crooke of the Destroyers,' he said, almost conversationally. Now his old fearful 'other ranks' voice was gone. Clearly he was a man used to command. 'For an Englishman you have shown surprising initiative in finding me. I was...'

'Hold your tongue!' Crooke cut in. 'Where's the bottle?'

Weed shrugged in the continental fashion, while the farmers stared at him and the intruders in blank incomprehension. 'I am afraid I don't know, *Lieutenant* Crooke.'

'You'd better remember,' Crooke snapped, 'because if you don't my first two bursts are going to smash your kneecaps. However much the medics may patch you up, you'll never walk another step.'

Crooke curled his finger round the trigger of his Sten.

Weed's eyes grew suddenly wary. 'Now, Crooke,' he said conciliatorily, the note of superiority gone from his voice. 'We can talk this out like gentlemen, can't we — *Los Piet!*'

'Look out, sir!' Thaelmann cried as a gigantic shape detached itself from the shadows.

Instinctively Crooke fired. At that range he couldn't miss. A spurt of flame shot from the muzzle of his Sten. The front row of farmers were bowled over, as if struck by some gigantic fist.

Crooke caught a glimpse of a broken-nosed, brutalized face. The next instant a ham-like fist smashed into his face. He staggered back. Blood spurted from his nose. A great sneering ox of a man in civilian clothes loomed up in front of him. The man hauled back his fist. Again it crashed into Crooke's face. He swayed on his feet. The giant's face shivered before him in a blurred mist. Numbly Crooke waited as the man brought back his fist again. Suddenly Thaelmann raised his Sten and fired a burst at the electric bulb in the ceiling.

At once confusion became chaos. The Yank cursed. A whiff of garlic-heavy breath struck Crooke in the face. It was the great, ox-like farmer. Crooke struck out wildly in the darkness. The farmer laughed. Sidestepping, he placed a big, hard palm in Crooke's face and pushed. Crooke went reeling through the confusion and crashed into the barn door. Slowly he began to slide to the floor.

'Mr Crooke — where are you?' It was Peters.

'Here — here,' he called weakly.

The next moment the farmer's weight descended upon him. His stale garlic breath struck him in the face, as his great hands sought and found Crooke's throat. Muttering triumphantly in guttural Flemish, oblivious to the confused fighting going on all around him, he started to exert pressure on Crooke's neck. Stars began to explode before Crooke in the darkness. A myriad colours, increasing in intensity every second, as he writhed and twisted frantically to escape that murderous grip.

Suddenly the giant farmer grunted hard. Crooke felt his grip relax momentarily. He gasped for breath. The grip tightened again. Far, far away a voice was crying in English. Something was striking the back of the giant's head. He could hear the metal thud against the solid bone and soft flesh. Over and over again! The man's grip relaxed. This time for good. The farmer fell to the floor at Crooke's side like a broken, crumpled doll, the back of his head smashed to pulp by the butt of the Guardsman's Sten.

For one long moment Crooke lay there, the man's feet sprawled over his legs. Gratefully he sucked in air as the fight diminished and died away. Then Peters was helping him to his feet, asking anxiously if he was alright.

'Thanks — okay,' he whispered hoarsely, 'get a light, will you.'

Thaelmann flicked on his torch. Yank hurried to the rickety table which bore the radio. He pushed aside the dead operator, slumped over his apparatus in a pool of blood, and lit the candle on the top of the radio.

Crooke looked around the barn. In one corner a group of frightened farmers stood with their hands raised high. The floor was piled with the dead and seriously wounded of Crooke's first burst. There was blood everywhere.

Crooke stepped over the crumpled body of the giant, with legs that felt like rubber. He stared at the farmers. Next to him Thaelmann curled his finger on the trigger of his Sten menacingly. The Flemings cowered back, as if they could already feel the lead penetrating their bodies.

Up the cobbled street there came the sound of many feet running towards the barn. The village had been aroused. Peters sprang to the door and opened it. 'They're coming!' he cried.

'Thaelmann,' Crooke said quickly, forcing himself to overcome the pain and nausea. 'Ask them where Weed is.'

Thaelmann pushed his Sten into the belly of a fat brick-faced elderly Fleming. 'Where is the German?' he commanded.

The man was so terrified, he could hardly speak.

The sound of heavy boots and clogs was getting closer. The Yank joined Peters at the door, machine pistol at the ready.

'He's gone,' the farmer stuttered finally. 'Through there.' With a hand that trembled violently, he pointed into the gloom at the back of the big, ancient barn.

From outside came the first of the explosions. A scream of agony cut the air, as the leading villager ran into the antipersonnel mines which the Guardsman had spread across the road.

'Get a load of that!' the Yank yelled excitedly. He squeezed the trigger of his Sten. The villagers flopped down. Flustered, inaccurate rifle fire began to come their way.

Hastily Peters crashed the door home. 'There's about fifty of them out there, sir!' he cried, as he and the Yank raced to the windows on both sides of the door. With the butts of their Stens, they smashed the glass and, thrusting aside the sacking coverings, they began to fire short, controlled bursts at the villagers outside.

Crooke knew he must act fast. Weed had gone, but where was he heading? He must find that out. He grabbed Thaelmann by the arm and thrust him towards a fat, elderly farmer. 'Ask him what Weed was going to do about Eisenhower.'

The farmer must have caught the name 'Eisenhower'. He waved a finger at them like a teacher at a naughty child. '*Nix Eisenhower — nix Eisenhower*,' he said urgently.

Thaelmann hit him with the butt of his Sten in the face. Something snapped in the man's nose. A great gob of blood spat onto the floor. The farmer's eyes started from his head with pain and fear. Blindly he sought his ruined nose. Thaelmann didn't give him a chance. Brutally he knocked the farmer's hand away. '*Talk!*' he yelled.

The farmer stared at him numbly, blood pouring down his face.

Thaelmann raised his Sten.

'*Nicht schlagen … nicht schlagen!*' the farmer cried piteously, raising his hands to protect his face. Crooke could see the orange V on the skin between his thumb and forefinger quite clearly in the flickering yellow light of the candle. '*Maar ik weet niet precies waar hij nu is*,' he quavered, relapsing into Flemish.

'He doesn't know exactly where he is now, but I do,' a younger man pushed forward through the terrified farmers. 'Leave my father alone — I'll tell you.'

'*Neen!*' the man's father protested.

The young man ignored him. He pulled a card out of his pocket and thrust it into Crooke's hand. 'There. We were waiting for orders from Germany. But that is where he was to go.'

Crooke glanced at the creased little card. 'THE ACE OF SPADES — GRITS, GREAT MUSIC — GREATER GIRLS.' Then the barn door blew in. The villagers were about to rush the place.

Crooke reacted. '*Come on — Yank and Peters!*' he yelled. He picked up his Sten and fired a burst at the ground, just in front of the cowed farmers. They sprang back, fighting to get clear. Behind him the two Destroyers retreated from the shattered windows. Another potato masher grenade sailed through the door and exploded. Its blast picked up the body of the dead giant and slung it unceremoniously against the wall. Yank and Peters dashed through the yellow smoke, firing as they came. Hastily they all backed into the far end of the barn. The first villagers came running triumphantly through the door. The Destroyers' concentrated fire caught them by surprise. The sheer weight of bullets flung them to left and right like so many broken puppets. Thaelmann found the rear door and his big foot crashed it open. The Destroyers retreated through it one by one, firing burst after burst at the men piling up at the main door. The Flemings kept coming, without any attempt to take cover. There were at least twenty of them piled up dead and dying now, blocking the path of the others.

The cold air struck Crooke in the face. He breathed it gratefully after the acrid odour of the inside of the barn.

Stevens popped out from behind an ancient farm cart. The muzzle of his Sten was glowing a dull red in the darkness. 'What now, sir?' he asked.

'We're getting out of this place — *bloody sharp*,' Crooke snapped.

'Did you get Weed?'

'No, dammit!' He ducked as a slug whined off the cart, showering them with wooden splinters.

'Where is the bastard?'

'Running like hell, if I'm not mistaken,' Crooke replied, firing another short burst at the Flemings. 'Like we're going to be in a minute.'

A potato masher sailed through the air. They ducked instinctively. A dull boom and mud, snow and pebbles splattered their bent heads. Muhammed flung his knife. The grenade thrower screamed and went down, clutching his hands to his chest, trying to drag the knife from it.

'And where's he running to, sir?' Stevens gasped.

'Where, Stevens? To where all good Americans go — when they die! Paris.'

THREE: THE BLACK CHRISTMAS

'Gentlemen, this is going to be America's Black Christmas.'
Oberleutnant Deschner of the German Abwehr, 25 December 1944

CHAPTER 19

The Intelligence Corps Sergeant, whom they had found asleep on their first visit to the Paris headquarters of SIS, passed round the bitter French coffee sullenly. 'We're out of sugar,' he said. 'I didn't have time to get to the Commissary.'

'Yer,' Stevens sneered. 'The way you move, mate, yer'll be late for your own funeral.'

Mallory shook his head sadly. 'Stevens, have you *no* respect for the presence of senior officers?'

'It's that zombie, sir. Gets on me wick, he does. I was just getting Betty Grable in between the sheets when he comes to tell me that you want to see us.'

'When you've finished this mission, Stevens, I'll personally pay for you to hook up with the most expensive prostitute in Paris,' Mallory said with a grin.

'Ay, I've heard that one before — when you've finished this mission,' Stevens said dourly. 'Go on, sir, pull the other leg — it's got bells on it!'

For a minute or two Mallory let them drink their coffee in silence. The Destroyers had had a bad forty-eight hours until Dawson had managed to contact them and smuggle them out of the Flemish countryside. With the exception of Crooke, they had all slept for twelve hours as soon as they had been assigned bunks at the SIS HQ; they had been too exhausted even to eat.

Dawson nodded to Philby, who was waiting to begin. 'All right, chaps, w-w-would you pay attention to me? I checked out this n-n-nightclub, the Ace o' Spades. It's a place patronized by black American s-s-soldiers working at the Versailles HQ, and a f-f-few from what the Yankees call the

COMZ, rear echelon troops. It's really an estaminet, t-t-tarted up a bit and run by a French communist. A b-b-black Sengalese in fact.'

'Thank you, Philby,' Mallory said, taking over. 'I talked to "C" on the telephone this morning while you were all sleeping. Project X is hotting up again, it appears. Our agents have discovered that Germany's leading atomic scientist, a man named Heisenberg — Werner Heisenberg, has moved to a little town in Southern Germany called Hechingen. There is nothing strange about that save that our air intelligence boys have noted a new plant near Hechingen, which *could* — I emphasize *could* — be used for the production of the weapon I've mentioned to you already. Can we put Heisenberg's presence there and the new plant together and come up with something? I don't know. But "C", the boys in Washington, and both the President and the PM have given us top priority.' He paused. 'Obviously they think so.'

'Yes,' Philby butted in, 'you can pull out all the s-s-stops. We've g-g-got to get that water back.'

'*And* protect the Supreme Commander,' Crooke said emphatically, not able to conceal his dislike of the stuttering senior MI6 agent. 'Don't forget that.'

'I won't,' Philby said. 'After all, he'll be P-P-President of the United States one day — if he survives.'

'But sir,' Thaelmann protested, 'how do we know that Weed made it to Paris? It was tough enough for us to get out of Flanders. He'd have the same problem with our checkpoints everywhere.'

'Nothing positive,' Mallory said. 'But the radio detection people report that there is a tremendous increase in the volume of clandestine radio traffic in the capital. Naturally it could originate from anywhere. The place is full of illegal transmitters

— too many for us and the French to control. After all most of the transmitters could be communist — and half the French BCRA is made up of Communists now. Why should they stop their own people?'

Thaelmann went red, but said nothing.

'However, one of the new call signs that the detector chaps have picked up in the last twenty-four hours goes like this.' He took a pencil out of his pocket and tapped it rhythmically on Philby's desk, while the Destroyers listened attentively. 'You recognize it, I hope? I haven't much of an ear for music.'

'Who's afraid of the bloody big bad wolf!' said Stevens.

'That's right. The tune that Weed's toy watch played.'

'But if you've picked up the call sign, why haven't you zeroed in on the bastard?' the Yank asked.

'I appreciate your concern, Jones,' Mallory said somewhat pompously. 'But the transmitter is moved about the heart of Paris for every fresh broadcast and the location apparatus the French have at their disposal is pretty ancient. Nonetheless, they're working on it. So, assuming that Weed is here, what are we going to do? Paris is too big and time too short for a full-scale search — even if we had the men to do so. No, we have to draw him out into the open, bait a trap into which he'll walk, we hope.'

'How?' Crooke asked.

'First of all we've got to let him see that we're here and on to him so that he'll be aware that his time is running out. Obviously we don't know where he is, but that card indicates he has some connection or other with Philby's nightclub. You and your chaps will have the honour of showing the flag at the Ace o' Spades this evening so that Weed will be aware of your interest.'

'What then, sir?' Peters asked politely. Of all the Destroyers he was the only one who still retained the other ranks' traditional respect for officers.

'We pull the same trick as we tried in Brussels. Dawson is pretty sure that the business with the double is still unknown to the Germans. It's one trick they haven't tried with their own leaders, as far as we know. There's a problem, however. Since this big spy and saboteur scare, it's pretty well known that Eisenhower has moved into the main SHAEF headquarters area for better protection. We've got to get him out of the compound back into his own house at St Germain. There he should be a much easier target for any assassination attempt. The villa used to belong to Field-Marshal von Rundstedt when he was German Commander-in-Chief in France. The Germans must know its layout backwards. At all events friend Weed should have no trouble in getting the details of the place from Skorzeny's HQ.'

'Are we talking about the real General Eisenhower, sir?' Peters asked.

'No, we're…'

Before Mallory could complete his answer there was a polite tap on the double door and the Intelligence Corps sergeant poked his head inside. 'The American chap from Colonel Dawson is here, sir,' he announced.

'Good, t-t-tell him to come in,' Philby stuttered.

'Good morning, gentlemen.' It was Corporal Stead, his broad face wearing a happy smile. Mallory turned to Peters again. 'As I was saying, Peters. No, not the real Supreme Commander of course. We'll use the bait again.'

'Bait?' Stead queried. 'What's that, Commander?'

'You, Stead.'

CHAPTER 20

'The Supreme Commander will see you now,' General Bedell Smith said sourly. 'And remember, you've got exactly ten minutes to state your case. Okay?'

Commander Mallory nodded. 'We'll remember,' he said as he passed through the eighteenth-century door of Eisenhower's office, accompanied by Crooke and Stead.

Eisenhower looked up from the pile of papers in front of him and stubbed his cigarette out in the heaped ashtray on the cluttered desk. He looked sick and worried; there were deep circles under his eyes.

'Hi Joe,' he said to the double who was now wearing corporal's uniform again. 'You're putting on some lard again, soldier.' But there was no humour in his voice. Crooke could guess why: the great German offensive had been going on for a week now and there were no signs that the Allies were containing it.

'Yessir. Thank you, sir,' Stead said, staring rigidly ahead.

'Okay, don't get offended,' Eisenhower said. 'Stand easy, corporal.' He looked at the two British officers. 'I recognise your faces — Algiers, isn't it? The Destroyers?'

Mallory pretended to be impressed. It was an old trick on the part of the brass — very easy to pull off when they had been briefed by their staff. 'That's right, General. The business with Mussolini last year.'

'And what brings you to me, gentlemen?' Eisenhower asked.

'General, the Germans are out to murder you.' Mallory said determinedly. Eisenhower showed no surprise.

'I know. The Provost Marshal's been keeping me under the wraps for the last three days. I can tell you, Commander, I'm good and mad at the whole goddamn thing. When this is all over, I'm going to order an inquiry, believe you me.'

'I can appreciate that, sir. But this time we must take the attempt seriously. We have it from a very reliable source that your life is in danger.'

'Commander, don't give me any of that gobbledegook! You Britishers and your reliable sources — let me have the real dope.'

Mallory indicated Crooke with a nod of his head. 'Lieutenant Crooke here of Naval Intelligence's special squad has positive evidence that a German named Deschner — alias Weed — has been sent to Paris to kill you.'

'Okay, if you know so much, where is he now?'

'We don't know exactly, General. All we know is that he's expected to turn up at a nightclub called the Ace o' Spades, out here in Versailles.'

Eisenhower looked up at Bedell Smith.

'A local place, General, used by the dogfaces,' he explained.

'So what's the deal?'

'We have a request, General.'

'It is?'

'That you leave your house in the Petit Trianon and that Stead should take your place.'

'And move into the main HQ? I'm already over there. That goddamn colonel who runs the provost section insisted. I thought the guy wasn't right in the head the way he went on about Skorzeny and his thugs.'

'No General,' Mallory interrupted gently. 'Not to the main HQ. If the Germans have contacts with this place through the

Ace o' Spades, they'll know your movements pretty well, I'm sure.'

'What, then?'

Behind the General, Bedell Smith looked at his wristwatch significantly. Mallory knew what that meant. 'Out of Paris altogether,' he said hastily. Eisenhower looked at him aghast. 'In the middle of the biggest doggorn offensive I've ever been faced with! What would you suggest, Commander Mallory — Washington perhaps!'

'No, General. Not to Washington, but to your weekend cottage near London — Telegraph Hill.'

'Commander Mallory, that's impossible! I'm surprised you even dare suggest the possibility.'

Mallory glanced down at his watch. 'Well, General, I knew you'd say that, and for that reason I asked someone else to call you and put my case forward.' He broke off. The green scrambler phone on Eisenhower's desk was beginning to ring, just as Philby had promised it would.

Eisenhower picked it up. Over his shoulder, Bedell Smith glowered at Mallory, his lips pressed together with pain. Obviously, Mallory thought, the Chief-of-Staff's notorious ulcers were acting up again: Philby had briefed him on the reason for Smith's chronically bad temper.

'You, sir?' Eisenhower said in surprise, when the operator put the call through. 'Thank you, sir. One moment please.' He placed his hand across the phone. 'Would you fellers go out into the other office for a minute.' As the Chief-of-Staff ushered them out, Mallory heard Eisenhower protest. 'But sir, I can't do that —'

But he could. Five minutes later when Bedell Smith ordered them back in again, the Supreme Commander was sitting numbly at his desk, his shoulders slumped in resignation. 'You fellers don't stop at anything, do you?' he said sourly, but there was a hint of admiration in his voice too. 'You really pulled rank on me this time — the Prime Minister himself!'

He turned to his Chief-of-Staff. 'You'd better pack your AWOL bag, Beetle.'

'What!'

'Yeah,' Eisenhower said a little wearily, 'Mr Churchill has invited us to Chequers for Christmas, with the approval and — to use the PM's own words — the warmest support of the President.' He shrugged. 'We go.'

He looked up at Mallory again. 'Okay, so you've got your way. I'm going. Incidentally Telegraph Cottage is out. Security says Chequers is safer and easier to guard. The big Skorzeny scare has reached the UK now. The good word is that all the German POWs there are going to break out of their cages at a given signal from Skorzeny's agents. So this is the deal. I'll fly out tonight. I'll arrange it that my staff thinks I'm going on a short hop to one of the frontline headquarters. Let's say Patton's advance HQ in Luxembourg City. I'll take the L-5 from here instead of my C-47 at Orly. When the L-5 comes back — from the front tomorrow morning — you'll be in it, Stead.' His irritation at the whole situation broke through. 'And if you don't watch that gut, soldier, you'll be eating yourself out of a nice safe job.'

'Yes General,' Stead muttered miserably, staring straight ahead, as if he could already see the truck coming to bear him to the front, and the short but not very sweet life of the average rifleman.

'One last thing, Mallory. I'm going to throw a total news blackout on my movements. Bedell, remember to get on to the PRD people at *Scribe*. Nothing on me from this evening onwards!'

'Yes General.'

'But remember, Mallory, I can't maintain the blackout for very long. There'd be too many goddamn rumours — and there are enough of them as it is. In other words, you've got to find the killer quick — very quick.'

'How quick, General?' Crooke asked, speaking for the first time.

'Forty-eight hours, that's all. On the morning of 26 December, I'm back in this office, working.' He waved a hand at them.

'Goodbye gentlemen.'

By the time they reached the door, the man who commanded the destinies of four million Allied soldiers was bent over his papers once more, working.

CHAPTER 21

The Destroyers started to drift into the Ace o' Spades at around nine that night. It was already an hour after the new curfew time which SHAEF had slapped on US troops in the Paris area as a result of the great Skorzeny scare, but the club was packed all the same with scores of American soldiers.

The long, narrow, typical *estaminet* with the raised platform at the far end for *le dancing* had been broken up by a series of little alcoves, now filled with drunken women and GIs whose brilliantined hair and faces glistened in the dusky red light.

The noise was terrific. On the little platform, a three-piece band of French Senegalese, cigarettes clamped between their lips, were playing *ball musette* music badly with much clashing of cymbals and beating of the big drum. At the bar itself, its top awash with beer suds, soldiers enjoyed themselves without restraint. The blue-smoke air was full of laughter and the wild giggles of the prostitutes.

Together, Yank, Muhammed and Stevens pushed their way through the throng. They reached the zinc-topped bar and elbowed a place next to a fat corporal with the AA patch of the 82nd Airborne Division on the shoulder of his combat jacket. The Yank clicked his fingers noisily at the big Senegalese bartender. Lazily he shuffled over to them. The Yank held up three fingers. '*Biere*,' he said with a poor attempt at the French word. '*Trois*.'

Stevens nudged Muhammed. 'Get a load of that. Our American cousin can talk the lingo.'

The fat Airborne corporal turned and looked at them curiously.

'Limey?' he queried.

'That's right chum,' Stevens said.

The Corporal opened his mouth to say something, but the look on Yank's glowering face told him it would be better not to. He turned away.

Sullenly the Senegalese pushed three glasses of beer across the counter at them. Beer spilled down the sides of the glasses.

Yank thrust a crumpled twenty-franc note at him.

The Senegalese picked it up and stuffed it carelessly into his pocket. He swished his dirty cloth across the counter. Beer ran across it and soaked the bottom of their glasses. The Yank looked at him angrily. The Senegalese grinned, showing filed teeth.

They turned and stared at the scene. At their side, the fat Corporal was amusing his listeners with a passable imitation of President Roosevelt's radio broadcast, declaring that he would never go to war: 'Mah good friends, ah hate wah. Sistie hates wah. Buzzie hates wah — we all hate wah. Ah'll never send yo boys ovahseas.' The Corporal dropped the Roosevelt voice. 'And where is we now, boys?' he asked scornfully. 'We's overseas and if we ain't careful, we'll soon be getting our nuts shot off!'

There was a burst of high-pitched laughter and much slapping of knees.

Muhammed dug Yank in the ribs. 'Look at that, Yank,' he said urgently, his eyes gleaming with lust.

A big-bosomed blonde, in high wooden platform shoes, tight black skirt that emphasized her curves and a white blouse from which her breasts threatened to burst loose at any moment, had staggered onto the platform at the end of the room. She shouted something at the Senegalese. They gave her a roll and a clash of cymbals. She began to sway back and forth in drunken excitement, a lock of blonde hair hanging down the side of her sweating face. There was a burst of catcalls and whistles. 'Shake it baby,' excited soldiers shouted. '*Shake it!*'

She needed no urging. The blonde was indulging herself in some private erotic fancy. The band joined in, picking up the tempo. She started to revolve her hips in time to the rhythm, the sweat pouring off her brow now, her eyes turned upwards, as if she had completely forgotten her suddenly excited audience.

Next to the Yank, the big Airborne Corporal cupped his beringed hands to his mouth and yelled: 'Take it off, lady!'

There was a burst of approval, followed by laughter throughout the room. Crooke, who had just entered with Peters and Thaelmann, stopped at the door, appalled apparently by the scene.

Without stopping her lascivious grinding, the blonde ripped open the front of her blouse and flung it away to reveal a gleaming black crêpe de Chine slip under which her big breasts moved as if they had a life of their own.

The audience yelled ecstatically.

The Corporal put his hands round his mouth again and shouted, 'More, lady, more!'

The drums were thudding faster now. The drunken blonde, her lips parted and her nostrils flared, lifted up one hip and ripped open the buttons of her skirt. She stopped momentarily and let it sink to the floor.

The spectators began to clap and whistle furiously. Her black shift ended just above her plump waist. She was naked below it, save for black silk stockings, rolled at the knees.

The Corporal flashed the Yank a look of triumph.

The blonde's whole body began to shake. Her plump belly moved in and out frantically. Her breasts shuddered. Sweat poured off her, as she began to mime the sex act in explicit detail.

The audience loved it. Their eyes bulged. Their hips swayed to the rhythm of the woman's motions.

Suddenly the blonde broke into great shuddering jerks, as if she were reaching a climax. She thrust her clenched hands back and forth against her stomach. Her legs straddled, her hips revolved in a mad circle. Meaningless words and groans fell from her slack lips.

'Shoot, you're like a lot of goddamn hogs in a trough of mash!' the Yank shouted at the top of his voice, lifted his glass of beer and threw it at the woman. She stopped abruptly. Behind her the band faltered, missed a beat and faded away.

The Airborne Corporal swung round. A knife gleamed in his fat beringed hand. 'You've been waiting for this, soldier, ain't you — ever since you came in! You wanted trouble. Well, you've got it now.'

His cronies scattered wildly. Suddenly there was a space around the Corporal and the Yank. 'AA — all American crumbs!' the Yank taunted him, but his face was tense and expectant.

The Corporal crouched lower, knife poised at the ready. Without taking his eyes off him, the Yank reached to his side and picked up a beer glass.

'Come on lads,' Stevens said helplessly, feeling the GIs crowd in on him and Muhammed, 'let's relax! Have another beer.' Desperately he cast a glance out of the corner of his eye, in the hope that the other Destroyers would come to their aid. But they were blocked by a silent but determined pack of American soldiers. In vain they tried to elbow their way through, but more and more GIs were getting in their path.

'I'm a combat soldier,' the Corporal said softly. 'Dropped in Normandy and in Holland. It ain't the first time I've killed a man. Them other times it was Germans. *Now it can be an American!*' He lunged forward rapidly.

At the last moment the Yank started back, as the gleaming blade missed his stomach by inches. He crashed the glass mug into the Corporal's face. The glass cracked in two.

Blood spurted from the Yank's knuckles, but the blow seemed to have no effect on the Corporal. He shook his head and brought up his knife again. The Yank sprang back. There were beads of sweat standing out on his brow now. He licked his lips and waited. The Corporal chuckled. His fat cheeks trembled with laughter, but there was no answering light in his eyes. Without taking his eyes off the Yank, he commanded, 'Watch his buddies! I don't want nobody to get between me and this guy here. He's mine!'

Suddenly a dozen arms grabbed Muhammed and Stevens. They tried to throw off their captors, but there were too many of them.

In the centre of the room, Crooke and the other two Destroyers were equally helpless, pressed in by a solid wall of GIs.

The Corporal crouched again, the knife held upright, almost level with his face. There was no sound in the *estaminet* now save the drip of the tap behind the counter and the soft sobs of the blonde woman sprawled on the stage. The Corporal took one step forward. The Yank tensed, his hands spread at either side of his body.

'*Stop that!*'

A black Tech Sergeant had come through the curtain that separated the bar from the backroom. In his hand he gripped a pickaxe handle, but his steady, penetrating gaze, born of

131

authority, indicated that he did not feel he would have to use it. 'Did you hear what I said?'

For a long moment nothing happened. The Tech Sergeant took a step into the room and stopped. 'I won't *ask* you again, Corporal.' He said in a clear voice, the threat undisguised. Slowly the fat Corporal relaxed his grip on the trench knife and it fell to the floor. The tension was broken. The Tech Sergeant put the pickaxe handle on the bar and smiled. 'Fine — that was a smart move, Corporal.'

Before the man could reply, he nodded to the men holding the Destroyers. They relaxed their grips immediately. On the stage, the Senegalese band began to play again. The drunken French woman staggered off to the *Cour*. The Tech Sergeant turned to the bartender and said something to him rapidly in French. Hastily he began to fill glasses of beer and slide them down the wet counter towards the Destroyers. The Tech Sergeant smiled again. 'For you fellers,' he said casually, 'on the house. Suds on the house — isn't that a pretty fine peace offering?'

Crooke pushed his way over to the Yank. 'What's going on, Jones?' he snapped.

'Just a little difference of opinion, sir,' the Tech Sergeant answered for the Yank. 'Always the same, I'm afraid, sir, with drink and wild-wild women.'

'Who are you?' Crooke rapped, turning to him.

'Technical Sergeant Joseph White, sir. I'm with the 202th Transport Battalion COMZ. I help out here of an evening when I'm off duty.'

'I see.' Crooke stared at the handsome NCO who stood opposite him in respectful silence. His features were perfect — high intelligent brow, keen clear eyes, perfect teeth, a strong, well-formed jaw. There was also a natural authority about the man, as if he were used to having his orders carried out promptly and without discussion.

'Thank you for the offer of the beer, sergeant,' Crooke said. 'But I think it would be better if we left at once. We don't want trouble.' The Yank sniffed and picked up his cap, wiping it free of the beer suds in an over-exaggerated demonstration of his contempt. If the Tech Sergeant noticed the gesture, his smiling handsome face did not reveal it.

'Perhaps it would be better after all, sir,' he said politely. As the Destroyers filed through the curtain into the blackout, he cried after them, 'And watch the step, sir! It's a bit dangerous.'

He waited till they had drawn the thick felt curtain closed, then he turned on the big Corporal. His pleasant polite manner was gone now.

He leaned over the bar and pulled the Corporal towards him with both hands. He brought his face to the Corporal's which had gone sickly-green with fear. 'Fatso,' he hissed, hardly able to control his rage, 'if you ever pull a crappy trick like that again, I swear I'll cut off your dong myself!'

Contemptuously he released his grip and let the Corporal stagger back. He swung round hastily and went through the curtain to the backroom and the telephone. He slipped a *jeton* in it and began to dial the number of the hotel. The Destroyers had turned up, as expected. Weed would want to know that important piece of news at once.

CHAPTER 22

'Did he see you come up the stairs,' Weed asked, a little anxiously, as White came through the door.

The Tech Sergeant shook his head. 'No, he was drunk as usual.'

Weed smiled and gestured White towards a moth-eaten easy chair. 'Good. I didn't think he would. As soon as he gets a few francs in his pocket, he's away.' He pointed to a half-empty bottle of Scotch on the bedside table. 'Help yourself.'

White shook his head. 'Never use it myself. Three point five American beer is about my limit.' He lowered his big frame carefully into the rickety chair and stared at the little German, dressed in shabby civilian clothes, complete with the dark ribbon of the *Médaille Militaire* in his buttonhole. It was, he knew, part of the German's cover which now identified him as Armand Schneider, Alsatian, wounded and invalided out of the Army in May 1940.

White showed his perfect teeth in a hard smile. 'A couple of times when I was a kid I thought I was for a necktie party. But when I was at Howard, I started to learn how to keep my nose clean.' He watched Weed take a deep drink of neat spirits and saw how his hand trembled slightly. Weed, he thought, was slowly getting close to breaking point. 'Yeah,' he said conversationally, 'in spite of what those fuddy-duddy Uncle Tom college professors said, I knew that I was going nowhere. You know, when they started the draft in '40, I was glad to receive my greetings from Uncle Sam. An M.A. in social anthropology from Howard and the best job I could get was bellhop or bus boy. Hell, I jumped at the chance to get into the

Army. I made tech sergeant in a year. Boy, wasn't I glad when the *Queen Elizabeth* left Pier Nineteen in '42 and I knew I was heading for Europe.'

Weed emptied his glass and sat up on the bed. 'You're not doing so badly. Head of the biggest black market ring in the COMZ area, running the whole Red Ball Express racket. Hell, White, you must be worth a fortune.'

'Well, I'm not hurting. As soon as I was posted to the Red Ball Express, I figured there was dough there. One truck of Class VI stuff sold on the Black Market — well, I guess you can figure what that would bring.'

Weed nodded. 'Yes, that bottle there cost me the equivalent of Armand Schneider's monthly pension on the Black Market.' He helped himself to another large drink.

White sniffed. 'So as soon as the set-up was organized, I went over the hill. The guys do the rest. I just rake in the dough.'

'In a way,' Weed said, 'I can't figure out why you're helping me.' He raised his free hand hastily as if to ward off any protest. 'Naturally, I'm not complaining. Gee, I couldn't have made it this far, if you fellers hadn't picked me up in Belgium and got me through the checkpoints! But hell, I'm an enemy of your country…'

White ran his hand over his closely cropped hair thoughtfully. 'This deal won't last for ever. Someone is going to get a snootful and shoot off his mouth in some cathouse or saloon. Then the MPs'll be on us like that!' He snapped his thumb and forefinger together loudly.

'So, I need papers and I need them now. I want out before the crap hits the fan.'

Weed rose from the bed and walked to the battered chest-of-drawers in the corner, unlocked the top drawer and took out a sheaf of documents. 'From Berlin this afternoon,' he said, 'courtesy the *Broederbond*'s courier. Brought them under a load of hothouse salad for the Christmas market. Hence the slight odour.'

White's eyes lit up when he saw them. 'They sure smell sweet to me,' he said enthusiastically.

Weed handed him the passport. 'The pass is genuine. Colonel Skorzeny's forgers just had to add the details. The Spanish and Portuguese visas are the real thing too.' He made the continental gesture of counting money with his thumb and forefinger. 'Our people down there helped to grease the wheels of progress a little.'

White chuckled. 'Yeah, it's an imperfect world, isn't it.' He looked at the passport. 'A real genuine Brazilian pass... Ricardo Jimenez, importer. That sound's good. I'll import myself, eh?'

Weed nodded and handed him the US bankbook. 'Fifty thousand dollars deposited in the First National, New York — and here's the flight ticket, clipper from Lisbon to Buenos Aires and the travel permit from Paris to Lisbon, via Madrid. All in perfect order, I can assure you. When we Germans do something, we do it perfectly.'

'Sure, sure,' White said, stowing the documents carefully in the inside of his jacket. 'I know — that's why you're winning the war.'

Weed's pale face flushed. 'The *Amis* are running all the way from Monschau to Echternach. A matter of hours and we'll be over the Meuse. With a bit of luck we'll be in Paris again soon.'

'Yeah, yeah,' White said easily, 'I believe you. Me, I'll be in Brazil, then. Ricardo Jimenez, importer. Okay, so these limeys, the Destroyers, have turned up, as you predicted they would.'

Weed caught himself in time; he knew he couldn't afford to offend the American. He needed White if he were to carry out his plan. 'Of course they turned up.' He sank down on the bed again. 'They wanted to provoke me into making a move — flush me out, I believe they call it in hunting circles. At all events they want me to make a move, which I will do — but at my convenience, not at theirs. What do you hear from your fellows in the Provost company?'

White was businesslike again. 'Eisenhower has moved back into his villa and out of the main compound.'

Weed nodded. 'As I expected. It's all part of their plan. They're trying to make it easy for me.'

'They've ordered a total news blackout about the big wheel's movements for the next forty-eight hours. But we've got a man who helps to service the big wheel's L-5. He heard the crew chief say that they could expect the plane back for servicing tomorrow morning. They all have to be on duty about eight. My guess is that Eisenhower is on a short visit to the line, coming back tomorrow morning, Christmas Eve. Otherwise he would have taken his C-47 at Orly Field.'

'Excellent, White, you're earning your fifty thousand dollars! That fits my plan exactly. Have you brought the gear with you?'

'The duds? Sure.' He indicated his musette bag in the corner. 'Both uniforms are in there.' He got up and fetched it. 'Here's the limey one.'

Weed nodded as he saw the red tabs. 'Just right.'

'And here's the other. The white gloves are at the bottom.' He looked up at Weed. 'The dye's in there too.'

Weed did not appear to hear. 'Okay, that's fine. Now let's explain the way I'm going to do it.'

When he was finished, White sat in silence for a moment, while Weed helped himself to another drink. His eyes were beginning to shine. Outside the streets were silent, broken only by the sound of a shunting locomotive at the Gare d'Austerlitz. 'Yeah,' White said at last, 'it sounds pretty good to me. You can have Fatso drive the jeep. He's a good guy. And I'll round up the others and give them the spiel. Poor guys. If they make it, okay. If they don't, as the French say, you've got to break eggs to make an omelette. Hell, all I'm concerned with is that I'm on that Paris train on Christmas Day, heading for Madrid. And you?'

'Me?' Weed chuckled drunkenly. 'I guess the whole of your Provost Corps will be out gunning for me — the guy who killed the Supreme Commander.'

White grunted. 'Why are you doing it? I'm in for the dough. But you?'

There was a long pause, then Weed said, 'Hate, just pure hate!'

It was just after midnight when Fatso drove the British Colonel up to the Eisenhower villa. It was snowing hard again, but the MPs, standing at the red-and-white striped barrier, were alert and tense in spite of the snow and the lateness of the hour.

A white-helmeted MP Sergeant stepped into the circle of yellow light and held up his gloved hand, his other crooked around the grease gun tucked into his side. The jeep crunched to a stop in the soft snow. 'Could I see your ED card, sir?' he said politely.

'Oh, course,' the British Colonel said. He relaxed his grip on the brown briefcase between his knees and reached inside his thick, tailor-made British warm.

The MP caught a glimpse of the red-tabs on his collar.

'And can I ask your business here, sir?' he inquired as he handed back the ID card.

'Courier from London, Sergeant. I've just got in from Orly. I've got an important communication for the Supreme Commander.' He indicated the brown briefcase. 'I know General Eisenhower won't be back till tomorrow morning, but I'll leave it with the Duty Officer. He can give it to Tex — er, Captain Lee. He'll see the Supreme Commander gets it first thing.'

'I see, sir,' the MP nodded, apparently satisfied by the explanation for this midnight visit. But he did not wave them on. Instead he stared curiously at Fatso. 'Say, how come you're wearing the 82nd patch?' he asked suddenly.

'I was in the 82nd, sir,' Fatso said. 'Wounded in Holland in September, sir. They shipped me out to the Orly Motor Pool, sir.'

'All right. Okay, sir, up the drive, take a right to the intersection and then take a left. The Duty Office is just behind the car park.'

'Thank you,' the Colonel said.

'And get that patch off,' he added, looking at the fat driver sternly.

'Yes sir,' the driver quavered.

The MP Sergeant saluted smartly and the jeep drove on slowly up towards the villa. Behind them the barrier came down again. Ten minutes later the jeep came out of the snow on the way back, the fat driver rigidly observing the 20 kilometre speed limit. As the jeep came level with the barrier, the driver stopped obediently. The MP threw a glance inside. The little Colonel was fast asleep, huddled up against the cold, his collar almost covering his face.

'Okay,' he said. 'And remember to get that patch off before I see you again.'

'Sure will, sir.' As he put the jeep into gear, he shouted, 'And a Merry Christmas to you, Sergeant!'

As the driving snow swallowed up the jeep, Fatso laughed wildly to himself, his whole body shaking with mirth. He jerked a big elbow into the sleeping Colonel's side. 'And a Merry Christmas to you too,' he chuckled, the tears streaming down his face.

Slowly the dummy lurched over and fell softly to the floor of the jeep.

CHAPTER 23

The little SHAEF Christmas Eve Party was a flop.

All the 'family', as Eisenhower liked to call them, was there: Kay, Tex, Butch, even the two dogs Telek and Caacie. But the knowledge that at this very moment thousands of young GIs were fighting and dying in the snowbound Ardennes weighed heavily on the guests.

The Destroyers, standing watchfully in the background, untouched drinks in their hands, eyeing the score or so SHAEF clerks and drivers who had been invited as well, could see that. In spite of the plentiful supply of bourbon from the Supreme Commander's own precious stock, there was a mood akin to despair about the proceedings.

The Versailles SHAEF headquarters was wild with rumours and frightening speculations. That morning, as they had walked down the long corridor to discuss the villa's security precautions with the Chief Provost Marshal, Mallory and Crooke had noted the little groups of grave-faced clerks and typists discussing the latest bit of alarmist 'scuttlebutt' in frightened undertones.

Even the colonel in charge of the MPs could not quite hide his fear that a whole regiment of heavily-armed German paratroopers might soon come floating down from the sky to attempt a suicidal attack on the villa. 'I'm glad to see you've got the situation well in hand, gentlemen,' he had told them hurriedly. 'But when it's a matter of the life of the Supreme Commander himself, that's not enough. We've got to beef up the defence organization. I'm gonna send you two Wasps.'

'Wasps?' they had queried in unison.

'Yes. You British produce them. They're Bren gun carriers mounting flame throwers.'

Thus a frozen Stead had been forced to spend an hour that afternoon watching a demonstration of the terrible weapons, until the two borrowed Wasps had been driven off to the stables used by the Destroyers and he had been able to escape to the warmth of the villa to prepare for the Christmas Eve party.

But both Mallory and Crooke knew that the news coming from the front was bad.

That morning SHAEF had heard that General Hodges, Commander of the US 1st Army, had been forced to evacuate his Spa headquarters because the Germans had already made their appearance in the suburbs. The news from Patton's 3rd Army front was not much better. Although he had promised Eisenhower that he would relieve the besieged American airborne troops at Bastogne by Christmas day, his men were still six miles away and taking a heavy beating on the one road open to them.

Eisenhower tried his best to enthuse some warmth and happiness into the SHAEF personnel, circulating from group to group and telling the same story over and over again. 'So when I'd briefed the commanders at Verdun on the extent of the German attack, Georgie got up and said: "Why don't we have the courage to let them sons-of-bitches go all the way to Paris and then we could really chew 'em up!"'

Most of his listeners laughed and remarked that it was typical of Patton but there was a hollow ring to their laughter, as if they felt that even he could not pull the US command out of the mess it was in at the moment.

In the end Eisenhower gave up. He refused another drink and everybody knew that he had given the signal for them to depart. Swiftly they downed their drinks and began to file out, shaking his hand formally and whispering 'Merry Christmas', without much enthusiasm. In five minutes the place was empty save for the Destroyers.

Stead waited till the servants had closed the doors behind them, then tugged at his collar and pulled off his tie. 'What a performance — and no one will ever know I gave it!'

Mallory, who had just come in through the side door, grinned. 'You'll make Hollywood yet.'

'In a pig's eye. All I want to make at this moment is a real stiff drink.'

Mallory looked at Stevens. 'Make him a real one, Stevens! We don't want our prima donna to get nerves at this stage of the game.'

Stevens winked and picked up the bottle of bourbon.

'And Stevens,' Crooke said warningly. 'Only for Stead — not for a certain cockney member of the Destroyers! We've got a long night in front of us, remember?'

'It's the rich what gets the pleasure,' Stevens commented and began to fix the drink.

Stead took it eagerly. 'The condemned man drank a hearty last supper,' he said. 'Okay, what does the tame fall guy do now?'

'You go to bed. All decent folks do at this hour,' Mallory said, lighting a cigarette.

'With a blonde?' Stead quipped. 'I thought all generals had rooms with hot and cold running maids?'

Mallory shook his head. 'Not this one. You'll be sleeping alone — save for those two beauties.' He indicated the Yank and Peters. 'They'll be in the room to your left. I'll be in the other, and we're all well armed.' He tapped the bulge in the pocket of his uniform significantly. 'And we'll be covering the outside,' Crooke added. 'There's a company of MPs in the grounds, but we'll be checking it at regular intervals to see that they're on their toes.'

Stead looked at Muhammed, Stevens and Thaelmann and then at their one-eyed CO. For a moment his easy-going manner vanished. 'When do you think he ... he'll come?' he asked hesitantly.

Crooke suddenly realized that Stead was a very brave man. The Destroyers were armed, trained and they could move about. Stead, on the other hand, was like a tethered goat, being exhibited openly as a prey for some marauding lion. 'I don't know, Stead,' he said softly. 'He could come at any time. But my guess is tomorrow morning. Possibly he'll work on the assumption that we'll relax our guard on Christmas Day. After all it is a day of rejoicing.'

Mallory smiled softly at Crooke's choice of phrase. 'Besides some of the MPs, he can assume, might have been drinking on Christmas Eve and will not be up to peak performance.'

Stead finished his drink with a gulp. 'Okay, then, gentlemen, so I'll hit the hay, I guess.' Carefully he fastened his collar and pulled up his tie in case any of the servants were still hanging on outside in the corridor. Slowly he walked to the door. They watched him go in sombre silence. Pausing at the big, gilt door, he said, 'If you shake me in the morning and I don't wake up, then you'll know he got me. Merry Christmas.'

'Merry Christmas, General!' they echoed in unison.

With that he was gone.

In the darkness, filled with the sour odour of bat droppings and ancient timbers, Weed crouched and waited.

Ignaaz Gerd Deschner, known to the *Abwehr* as 'the doctor', had come a long way for this appointment. For in essence, his whole life had been a long training for what would happen in the next two hours.

He had never seen his father. In the month that he had been born, August 1914, *Oberleutnant der Reserve* Deschner had marched away with his Swabian infantry regiment and never come home again.

Surprisingly enough in a war when the average life expectancy of an infantry lieutenant was three weeks, he survived three years before he was promoted to a staff job at divisional HQ. One day after the armistice had been declared, on the morning of 12 November 1918, *Oberst* Deschner crossed no man's land on the Franco–Belgian border to discuss the terms of his division's withdrawal with his American opposite number. But he never reached the US trenches. As his father's comrades told his mother later, when the division marched back to flag-bedecked Stuttgart to be disbanded, the *Oberst* had been shot down cold-bloodedly in broad daylight by a drunken Yankee lieutenant, who had just been posted to the front and missed all the fighting. 'Shot down in cold blood in broad daylight', was one of the first sentences he remembered his mother ever saying.

'On the first day of peace by the Yankee murderers!'

Throughout his youth, the lonely, undersized boy's hatred of those 'Yankee murderers of your dear father' had been nurtured by his mother, trying to eke out a living on the miserable pension the Weimar Government granted them. For him the '*Sammies*', as they were called, were all 'gangsters', 'terrorists' and 'degenerate cowboys'. Yet, surprisingly enough, when the only chance to continue his studies was to go to Yale for a year in 1938 on an American scholarship, he found he liked Americans.

They were open, hospitable and kind. For the poor provincial Swabian student, whose life had been centred on his mother and his books up to then, America had been an eye-opener. For the first time in his life, Deschner had begun to enjoy himself, going out to parties, 'on dates', fraternity 'bull sessions', helped along by countless bottles of weak beer.

In 1939, when Germany went to war, he hurried home on the *Bremen* to volunteer, but instead of joining the infantry like his father, he applied for the German secret service, *Die Abwehr*. He had no intention of fighting against his American friends. Admiral Canaris had welcomed such a brilliant linguist with open arms, nicknaming him '*der Herr Doktor*', though Deschner had never finished his doctorate.

Between 1939 and 1942, he served on many fronts in many guises — an Alsatian bricklayer's labourer on the Maginot Line in 1939–1940, a Baltic horse-trader on the Russian–Lithuanian frontier in early '41, a Maltese merchant in Cairo in the spring of '42. Then the urgent summons had come from the *Abwehr* HQ in Berlin's Tirpitzstrasse; something had happened to his mother in his native Stuttgart. He must return at once.

The family doctor had ushered him into the room where the body had been placed and consoled him with the fact that her death must have been instantaneous. Numbly he had insisted on seeing the body. Doctor Deutschle had hesitated but in the end had shrugged and pulled back the white sheet. Where his mother's face had once been there was a bloody stump sticking up from the rumpled, black dress. The bomb had taken her head off!

'Who was it?' he asked thickly after Doctor Deutschle had escorted him into the fresh air. 'The Royal Air Force?' The aged doctor shook his head. 'No, the *Amis* — the Americans.'

A wave of hatred flooded over him. Twenty years before the *Amis* had killed his father; in 1942 they had returned to kill his beloved mother. Now he saw those laughing, open, easy-going people he had known at Yale in 1938 for what they really were — unthinking automatons, who killed from afar with their machines, safe from any form of retaliation. Remote murderers, they had slaughtered his father with a sniper's rifle and now his mother with a Flying Fortress. That day in Stuttgart he swore he would have his revenge on the *Amis*, who had fooled him so easily with their glittering, open-handed world.

Two days later he volunteered for the *Abwehr's* section dealing with North America and threw himself into the work heart-and-soul. The sexual seduction of American POWs so that they would spy on their comrades, the blackmail of US businessmen who had not been too careful in their business deals with Europe, the bribing of American consular officials in Europe to reveal diplomatic secrets — no job was too dirty for *der Doktor*. But throughout the years since his mother's brutal death at the hands of the '*Ami* air terrorists', as he sank deeper and deeper into the morass of the 'department of dirty tricks', as the *Abwehr* called his section, where he learned that everything and everyone had a price, he longed for a clear-cut, decisive intelligence mission.

Obersturmbannführer Otto Skorzeny had given him the opportunity to get out of the 'dirty tricks department'. Just as the gigantic, scar-faced SS Commando's rescue of Mussolini from the Gran Sasso in 1943 had changed the course of the war, his new assignment, he realized immediately, could do the same. With Eisenhower out of the way, the great Allied coalition would fall apart. The Führer would have time to deal with the Russians before the Allies could reform a united front.

By then, the Führer would be in a powerful enough position to negotiate a suitable peace with the Western Allies. Perhaps Germany might lose some territory; but that would be infinitely better than the indignity of the Allied demand for 'unconditional surrender'. But, as Weed nodded off to sleep, his mind was not concerned with the future consequences of his actions; solely with the urgent desire to liquidate the man who was the chief representative of the *Amis* in Europe. The General who was worth ten divisions to the Allies must die to atone for the death of a lowly German infantry colonel who had been killed nearly a quarter of a century before and a homely Stuttgart housewife, one of several thousand other housewives killed that day.

Just after four, he awoke. He was awake immediately, fearful that he had slept too long. He got up quickly and, taking care to make no noise, crossed to the window. It was still snowing outside. 'Keep it up Frau Holle,' he said, thinking of the legend of his schooldays, 'keep shaking the beds.'

Noiselessly he padded back to his sleeping bag. In the thin grey light he began his preparations. One by one he took the items from his AWOL bag: the two aluminium tubes, the small compact electric battery, the five explosive bullets.

Swiftly he fitted the murder weapon together, with practised fingers that needed no light to guide them. He squeezed the smaller tube which acted as a trigger. There was a soft hiss of compressed air. Nodding with satisfaction, he loaded the bullets carefully and placing the little electric gun down, reached in his bag again to pull out the bottle. 'My insurance policy', he whispered in English, speaking to himself like so many lonely men.

He had just finished when he heard the unmistakable sound of a jeep labouring over difficult terrain. He rushed to the window and forced it open. Narrowing his eyes, he peered into the darkness and saw a blue pinprick of light from a blacked-out torch. Once — twice — three times. It was White. He was in position with his jeep. As soon as the firing started, he would drive up to the eastern wall. They had agreed White would wait there for exactly five minutes. If he didn't make it, White was to leave. He had done his bit and could enjoy his new identity and fortune without interference.

Slowly Weed returned to his sleeping bag. His escape route was secure. Now all that was lacking was the diversion. He looked at his watch again, resisting the temptation to play the absurd little gadget. It was four-thirty. In thirty minutes — forty at the latest — they would be arriving.

Contentedly he stretched back on his khaki sleeping bag and, placing his arms underneath his head, tried to penetrate the gloom above him. The old house was silent. Everyone was asleep. Tomorrow, only the most essential personnel would have to go on duty; after all it was Christmas Day. They could sleep late. No six o'clock calls this morning. He chuckled to himself.

The men sleeping below who survived the next hour would remember this Christmas Day for the rest of their lives. 'Gentlemen,' he said to the darkness, 'this is going to be America's black Christmas!'

CHAPTER 24

Crooke woke with a start. Instinctively his hand flew to the pistol which lay beside him. But it was only Thaelmann, fumbling around in the darkness of the stable opposite the guardroom. The German switched on the light. His shoulders were covered with snow.

Crooke licked his lips. 'What time is it?'

'Nearly five, sir. I wasn't going to wake you for another five minutes.' He slumped down on the cot next to Crooke's. In the corner Muhammed continued to snore, his mouth wide open. 'It's snowing like the devil outside, sir.' He bent down and started to pull off the clumsy, black-felt overshoes which the American MPs had loaned them. 'Stevens is in the guardroom, sir, with that American sergeant.'

Crooke nodded. He yawned and started to pull on his own boots. Thaelmann pulled the rough blankets over him. Before Crooke could get his overcoat on, he was fast asleep. As Thaelmann had said, it was snowing like the devil. But in spite of the driving flakes, the guards posted round the villa were alert. Crooke was checked twice, his face, pale and unshaven, being examined by the hissing light of a Coleman lamp. Just outside the guardroom, covering the main gate, the machine gunners crouched over their twin 50s like grey ghosts, their only movement the regular flick of a gloved hand to wipe away the snowflakes from their frozen faces.

Crooke opened the door of the guardroom and felt the heat from the stove in the corner hit him in the face. The MP Sergeant got up when he saw Crooke. 'Morning, sir,' he said lazily. 'Freeze the balls off yer out there. Pity the poor guys up the line.'

Crooke nodded. 'Any of that coffee going, Stevens?' he asked. 'Oh, and a happy Christmas to both of you!'

For a few minutes Crooke sat in silence, nursing his coffee, listening to the NCO as he detailed the events of the next few hours. 'SHAEF courier'll come in with the latest intelligence summaries in about ten minutes or so, depending on what the roads are like from HQ. And we're expecting a load of coke for the boilers between five and six. It's a regular run. The truck'll call at the Versailles Officers Club first and then they'll come to us.'

'Check it all the same,' Crooke ordered, sipping his coffee slowly, and then sank into a contemplative silence. Slowly he ran the problem through his brain once more.

It was obvious that Weed would know of the security measures at the villa by now. It followed that he would attempt something at a time when their security was at its most relaxed — Christmas Day lunch, perhaps? He knew the MPs were looking forward to their turkey and cranberry sauce 'and all the trimmings', as they had rhapsodized the night before in the guardroom. After twenty-four hours of guard duty, they deserved the change from the usual diet of soya links and brown stew.

But if the lunchtime period was the one Weed would select, how would he get in? The front gate was obviously out. It was far too heavily guarded. He would have to find some other way. The sewer system? Crooke remembered that he had read something about the gigantic sewers underneath Versailles somewhere or other; and the Poles had used Warsaw's system during their vain defence of the capital against the Germans a few months before. Could that be it?

A red-faced MP put his head round the door. 'Jeep and a truck coming up, Sarge!' he cried.

Crooke snapped out of his reverie. He rose to his feet as the NCO seized his helmet liner. 'Let's go see,' the latter said. 'Ya never know.' The two Destroyers followed him out into the snow. Outside, in the light of the Coleman, half-a-dozen MPs surrounded a jeep with a two-and-a-half-ton truck behind it. The NCO unslung his tommy gun purposefully. 'Okay, buddy,' he said to the driver of the jeep, 'get out'.

A heavily muffled figure, his face unrecognizable behind his khaki scarf, helmet liner and looted German goggles, said angrily: 'What gives? I'm the SHAEF courier. I always does this route.'

'Sure and I'm Clark Gable,' the Southerner drawled. 'Okay, haul ass.' He levelled his machine pistol. 'And quick — it's goddamn cold out here!'

With a muttered curse, the driver struggled out of the jeep and stood facing them. The MP flashed his torch on his face. 'Get them goggles off, and that scarf,' he ordered. 'I'd like to see your handsome mug.'

'Have a heart, Sarge. This weather would freeze the balls off a brass monkey.'

'Move it!'

Grumbling under his breath, the driver removed his face covering and stood shivering in the icy cold, his breath fogging the air.

'Okay,' the NCO said, 'I've seen you before. Take off.'

'Same old goddamn Army game,' the driver muttered and got back into his seat. With an angry clash of gears, he moved off, sending the jeep slithering in the new snow.

The truck came level with the barrier and stopped obediently in the pool of light. A black face peered down at them from the cab. 'Okay, come on down,' the sergeant commanded.

Dutifully the driver dropped down into the snow. He was a big man, a head taller than the NCO, with big hands that would have done credit to a prize fighter. 'All right, turn your face to the light and let's have your helmet liner off — move it!'

The driver looked down at the MP Sergeant. 'I'm a noncom,' he pointed to the three gold stripes on the sleeves of his dirty combat jacket. 'Buck sergeant.'

'Sure. Are you delivering the coke?'

The driver thrust a paper into the MP's hands. 'The work order. Two zero three transport company.'

The MP Sergeant opened his mouth to say something, but Crooke was quicker. 'Is there anybody else in the back of the truck, sergeant?'

'Yes, sir.'

'All right, tell them to get out. We want to see their faces.'

'Some kind of check?'

'Yeah,' the MP Sergeant answered, 'and for Godsake move it!'

Slowly and insolently the big driver walked to the back of the truck and beat on the canvas with his gloved hand.

'Okay you guys. Hit the deck. The boss man wants to see ya pretty faces.' From within came the sound of sleepy groans and curses. The canvas was flung back and the men who had been sprawled out on the coke dropped into the snow.

'Okay,' the MP snapped, 'line up and get your ID cards ready!'

Staring aggressively at each one of the young GIs he passed down the ragged line. Shivering in the cold, Crooke followed his progress. Suddenly the MP stopped in front of a fat corporal who was older than the rest of the men. 'Ain't I seen you somewhere before, soldier?' he enquired, holding the Coleman lamp higher so that he could survey the man's face better.

The fat corporal shook his head. 'No sir, you ain't seen me before. I ain't never been here before.'

The MP frowned. 'Could have sworn…'

'Sergeant,' Crooke cut in. 'I've seen that man. He was…'

He broke off. Behind him he heard the click of the pin being pulled out. He swung round. The driver of the truck had a dark object in his hand. '*Look out!*' Crooke yelled and flung himself backwards.

The grenade sailed over his head and landed inside the open door of the guardroom. As Crooke fell into the snow, he caught a fleeting glimpse of the MPs' contorted features. In the next instant the grenade exploded in a vicious flash and the guardroom was full of dead and dying men.

Fatso thrust his knife into the MP's belly and ripped it upwards savagely. As the Coleman lamp fell to the snow, the MP's knees buckled under him. 'Try that one on for size,' Fatso chuckled and, pulling out his knife, let him fall.

The GIs were galvanized into action. The driver jumped back into the cab and roared forward towards the house. Behind him, the rest of them started to back towards the same place, firing their pistols as they went.

Crooke pressed his body deep into the snow as the lead hissed through the air above him. To his right the door of the stable was flung open. Stevens stood there, tommy gun in hand. He fired a wild burst and missed. Next moment he ducked back as the concentrated fire from the GIs' pistols ripped the door to shreds. Wood and brick splinters flew everywhere.

The truck drew up with a squeal of brakes. Two men flung themselves out into the snow. Obviously they had been hiding beneath the coke. Hurriedly the driver pulled the blackout covers from his headlights. Their twin beams cut into the night, illuminating the whole length of the drive. A moment later Crooke saw why. The two men were setting up a machine gun, while the first group doubled past them into the house.

They managed it just in time, as a handful of MPs from the other guard post came panting round the side of the villa. Red tracer cut the air. The MPs didn't have a chance. The first man screamed and dropped at once, his legs shot from under him. Another skidded to a violent stop behind him and sank to the snow without a sound. Two more MPs piled up behind them. In an instant all was murderous confusion, with the machine gun chattering on remorselessly.

Crooke seized the opportunity offered him. He sprang to his feet and sprinted frantically for the protection of the stable. Stevens came panting after him, zig-zagging wildly like a professional rugby player.

Just as they made the door, the gunners turned on them. Lead chipped the brick and wood all around them, showering them with debris. Crooke flung himself inside, landing in a heap at Thaelmann's feet, as he crouched against the wall. Stevens followed the next instant, sprawling out full length in the straw.

'We couldn't knock,' he gasped, raising his head and grinning at the German. 'Hope you don't mind?'

Thaelmann grunted and ducked as a bullet shattered the window above his head.

Muhammed scuttled over to the little group at the door.

'What has happened, sir?'

Crooke knocked the snow off his elbows and knees. 'Weed started earlier than I anticipated,' he said grimly. 'This business is all part of his plan, I'm sure of that. But he wasn't among the men in that truck, I had a good look at them before the balloon went up.'

'Well, where the hell is he then?'

'He can't expect to get inside the villa now with all this racket going on,' Thaelmann said. 'The whole neighbourhood must be awake. He'd never get through.'

'There's only one explanation,' Crooke said slowly, as the full terrifying realization dawned on him. 'Those chaps are just a diversion. You know where Weed is?'

The three Destroyers shook their heads in silence.

'He's been here all the time, right under our noses.'

'But where, sir?'

'Inside the villa!' Crooke answered slowly.

CHAPTER 25

Noiselessly Weed doubled down the dusty stairs from the attic. At the bottom he opened the door carefully. No one. The corridor was empty as White had predicted it would be. The top floor was not used at all. Swiftly he moved down the corridor, sticking to the shadows along the wall. Now he could hear the steady chatter of their machine gun quite clearly. Soon they'd be fanning out into the ground floor to look for the 'fortune in dollar bills', which White had fooled the gang of deserters and black marketeers into believing the Supreme Commander kept in the villa.

As he moved purposefully towards his victim, he laughed to himself at their credulity. But he knew they had implicit trust in White, who had run the gang so successfully over these last three months. Besides they were providing a useful diversion at the moment. Naturally the guards would gun them down when they left the cover of the house, but by then he and White would be gone.

He paused at the top of the flight of stairs which led to the second floor where Eisenhower had his bedroom. He could hear the would-be looters shouting excitedly to one another on the ground floor as they ran from room to room. But there was no sound coming from the second floor. He could guess why. The brass would be cowering under their beds, scared out of their wits by the shooting outside. Swiftly he doubled down the stairs, three at a time. Before him the long corridor, which led to the Supreme Commander's room, lay empty. Eisenhower's room was at the end of the corridor. He had noted its location the night before when he had slipped away from the kitchen during the height of the Christmas Eve party and hidden himself in the attic. But where were the Destroyers? He did not want to get involved with them. Berlin had briefed him well enough on their reputation before he had seen them in action in the Ardennes. They were tough men. He wanted to carry out his mission swiftly and silently and get away while those fools down below kept the MPs occupied.

Just before he reached Eisenhower's room, he made a sudden change of plan. If the Destroyers were guarding the Supreme Commander, the firing would have alarmed them into running to protect him. The General's neighbours would undoubtedly have done the same. It was reasonable to assume that the rooms on either side of his bedroom would be empty. That would be his way in. Not through the door. They'd be expecting that. But across the large balcony which linked the two rooms.

Carefully he eased open the door. It moved without noise. In the far corner of the room the two cots were empty, the khaki blankets in disarray, as if the men who had occupied them had thrown them back in a hurry and jumped out. Silently he padded through the room to the tall French window. He tried the catch. It, too, opened easily.

He stepped out, the deep snow effectively deadening any sound. He glanced into the courtyard. The snow was littered with still, dark shapes. The bodies of the MPs were scattered everywhere. Here and there an MP scuttled from position to position among the cover of the outbuildings, but the two men at the machine gun were still keeping the survivors pinned down. The villa was sealed off completely.

Crouched below the level of the elaborate wrought-iron balustrade he worked his way carefully to the Supreme Commander's room. Hesitantly he peered through a slit at the side of the heavy, felt blackout curtain, his deadly little electric pistol held in a hand that was beginning to perspire freely.

It was as he had guessed. Eisenhower and his guards were there. Bathed in the yellow light, they were frozen into tense melodramatic postures like characters in a cheap play who had just received alarming news. Eisenhower, wearing a striped gown, had a big Colt in his hand, as did the naval officer standing protectively at his side. On both sides of the door, the two Destroyers — Yank and Peters — crouched at the ready, submachine guns tucked into their sides. Obviously none of them reckoned with the fact that the would-be assassin might come in from the window; it was too high from the ground.

Weed licked his lips and drew a deep breath. With all his strength he crashed his booted foot home against the central window frame. The wood splintered at once. The door flew inwards. He thrust aside the heavy curtain and fired in the same instant.

His bullet missed Eisenhower by inches and exploded on the wall behind him, showering the General and the naval officer with brick and plaster. Weed cursed. Moving into the room, he yelled: 'Put those hands up — quick!'

The two Destroyers spun round. 'It's him,' Peters yelled. 'You bastard, I'll…'

'You'll do nothing! Get those hands up — *now*!'

Reluctantly the four men dropped their weapons and raised their hands, staring at the intruder in GI uniform, with his strange and deadly weapon.

'You can't get away with it,' Mallory said, trying hard to sound calm. 'There's no chance of you getting out of here alive!' Even as he said the words, he realized just how absurd they were; Weed held all the aces.

'I shall kill you, General,' Weed said calmly enough, as if he were talking about the weather. 'And then I shall kill you three.'

'It's really not worth it,' said Mallory slowly, his voice a model of civilized composure. 'This man is not General Eisenhower. He's simply a double.'

A look of alarm crossed Weed's face. 'What?'

'You heard what I said,' Mallory answered quietly. 'The real Supreme Commander is in London. This man is just an actor.'

But the look on Weed's face told Mallory that he was wasting his breath. Weed laughed hollowly. 'That man is General Eisenhower. Why otherwise all the preparations — the guards, the party, everything? You can't fool me that easily.'

Stead laughed weakly. 'My best role. The only time in my career when I've sold anyone on my performance.' Weed raised his strange pistol again. It came level with his heart. Slowly the muscles of Weed's jaw hardened as he prepared to fire.

CHAPTER 26

It was Stevens who had the brainwave as they crouched in the stable in frustrated impotence, listening to the thwack and whine of the bullets striking the wall. 'There is a way out, sir! Why didn't I think of it before? We *can* get through them with the machine gun!'

Crooke stared at the cockney's excited face. 'How?'

'The Wasp!' He pointed to the dark outline of the little carrier at the back of the stable.

'Of course! Stevens, you're a bloody genius!' He sprang to his feet, heedless of the danger. 'What are we waiting for?'

With frantic fingers they tore at the ropes holding down the canvas. Even before they had pulled it back, Stevens had sprung into the driver's seat. Hurriedly he pressed the starter button. Crooke slipped into the narrow compartment next to Stevens. Behind him Thaelmann and Muhammed crouched behind the flame thrower. 'Okay, Stevens, let her go!'

Stevens flung the little carrier forward. It struck the stable door with a crash, and the Wasp rolled into the open. As Stevens swung her round in a ninety-degree turn to face the machine gun, Crooke yelled to the two men behind him, 'Fire at once!'

He ducked instinctively as the machine gun opened up at them. There was a sudden awesome whoosh. A searing flame shot out of the cannon. But the range was too far. It disappeared as suddenly as it had come, leaving a great black scorch mark in the snow.

Frantically the gunners fired at the little carrier. Tracer bullets zig-zagged through the air. Still Stevens pressed home the attack, clinging to the wheel as the Wasp bumped and jolted over the snow-covered garden, crashing through the ornamental bushes.

Crooke stood up, oblivious of the bullets, and yelled to Thaelmann and Muhammed crouched in the back. '*We're in range — fire now!*' He ducked as Thaelmann pressed the trigger.

A great flame shot out of the cannon. An oily, yellow flame ringed the gunners. Their terrible screams rang out above the crackle of burning and the firing stopped.

The Wasp rattled on past the twisted machine gun. In the circle of melting snow around it, two charred, unrecognizable figures lay crouched, as if praying. Behind Crooke, Muhammed and Thaelmann gasped with utter horror and turned their heads away quickly.

The Wasp hit the bottom step of the great stairs with a jolt. From within the house a ragged volley of small arms fire struck the stonework all around them. An ornamental vase fell from its plinth and shattered. '*Fire!*' Crooke yelled, as they clattered up the steps in first gear.

Thaelmann pressed the trigger again.

Once more the flame shot out. Suddenly the snow lodged above the door steamed and disappeared. The woodwork blackened and blistered as the paint began to burn. What was left of the glass in the windows splintered and clattered to the steps.

Crooke raised himself and yelled: 'Come on out! The next time we'll fire through the window. *Out!*'

The door was flung open. The panic-stricken men came pouring out, hands raised above their heads.

'Look out, sir!' Thaelmann yelled.

A bullet whipped off the front of the Wasp, a few inches from Crooke's stomach.

As he ducked, Thaelmann fired.

Fatso screamed as the flame set his clothing afire. He dropped his carbine. With the flame licking at his body, he ran wildly up the great stairs leading to the second floor. Dropping from the Wasp, the Destroyers ran after him.

As Weed prepared to fire, the door swung open. Fatso stood there swaying, his charred claw of a hand, from which the burned flesh hung in strips, held out in front of him, his face a mess of hideous purple and black blisters. Little tongues of flame still licked the bottom of his body.

For a moment Weed was unable to move.

Fatso staggered blindly into the room, his blackened claw pawing the air. 'Sergeant White?' he whispered hoarsely.

The Guardsman looked at the Yank aghast. 'He's blind,' he croaked. The dying man advanced between them, feeling his way towards the little German. 'Sergeant White — help me, *please!*'

Weed's face blanched with horror. Almost without knowing it, he squeezed the trigger of his gun. The explosive bullet hit the corporal squarely in the face. It disappeared in a ball of red flame. Blood spattered everywhere. Fatso shot backwards through the door, leaving what was left of his head on the carpet at the Destroyers' feet.

The Yank came to life abruptly. With a roar he launched himself forward. But he was unlucky. His foot slipped on the bloody mess and he crashed forward at Weed's knees. The little gun clattered to the floor, shaken out of the German's hand by the shock of the sudden attack.

'Get him!' Mallory yelled.

Weed started back.

From outside there came the sound of heavy feet running up the stairs. Frantically Weed rummaged in his jacket, his eyes distorted with fear. As the Destroyers came panting into the room, he pulled out the bottle.

Mallory reacted at once. 'Stay there!' He commanded. 'Is that it?'

'Yes — the sample,' Weed gasped, his gaze flicking from one face to another. 'And you know how important it is.'

Mallory took a step towards him, holding out one hand like a fond parent trying to coax something out of a stubborn child. 'Give it here, Weed, that's a good chap.'

Weed fought for control. 'I'm ready to cut my losses,' he said, his breathing calmer now. 'I failed. Now I want out.'

'What do you mean?' Mallory asked.

'I want my freedom to the wall of the villa. Let me get that far and you'll have your precious bottle then.' He pressed home his advantage.

'I could break it now.' He raised the bottle threateningly. 'But if you give me your word as a British officer that you'll wait in here till I reach the wall and order the MPs out there to let me through…'

'But sir, you can't let the little swine get away with it,' the Yank protested, picking himself up from the floor.

'I am afraid there's nothing else I can do, Jones,' Mallory said quietly.

Weed smiled. 'Good for you. Now call to those MPs down there and tell them I'm coming out.' Boldly he pushed past the Destroyers, bottle held high above his head so that they could not snatch it, and halted at the door. 'Now — please.'

Helplessly, Mallory strode to the window. 'Listen out there,' he yelled. 'I'm speaking in the name of the Supreme Commander! A man dressed in GI uniform is going to leave this building in a few seconds! You are not to hinder him in any way! Do you understand? *This is an order!*'

From below came a few half-hearted acknowledgements.

Weed allowed himself a smile. 'I have your word of honour, Remember!'

He turned and stepped carefully over the headless body slumped against the door.

'But the bottle?' Mallory said.

'As soon as I reach the wall, I shall place it there in safety. You can collect it when I've gone.' And with all assurance in the world, he began to walk along the corridor, the vital sample in his hand.

In silence they listened to the sound of his combat boots as he got further and further away. 'But you can't let him get away with it!' the Yank cried, his face suffused with rage. 'He killed the guy in the wood, he…'

He broke off as Mallory turned his back on him.

The Yank swung round at the others. 'But this is the goddamn twentieth century!' he yelled desperately. 'We're not playing cricket at them fancy-pants public schools of yours! This is war! I didn't give my lousy word!'

'*Jones!*' Crooke shouted and tried to block the Yank's path. Savagely Jones elbowed him in the stomach.

'*Yank!*' Peters yelled as he dived forward. '*For Christ's sake!*'

Too late. The Yank opened the window and, before anyone could stop him, had clambered on to the snowy balustrade. For a fleeting second, he hovered there, swaying back and forth wildly. Then with a great yell, he dropped straight on to the confident little figure marching across the snow beneath.

The Destroyers scrambled on to the balcony and stared down at the two still figures sprawled out on the snow, one on top of the other. Neither moved.

As the blood began to spread out around the bodies, they could just catch the metallic strains of *Who's afraid of the Big Bad Wolf?*

CHAPTER 27

'Would you have believed your sodding eyes!' Stevens exclaimed, as they closed the door of the hospital room behind them. 'To get away with a ruddy fool trick like that!'

Peters chuckled softly as he thought of the Yank's appearance. 'I bet them nurses is going to have a bloody awful time with him the next few weeks. Him with his legs stuck up in the air in that plaster like ready money!'

Thaelmann shook his head in disbelief again. 'Who would have thought it possible? The Yank gets a fractured wrist and two broken legs. Weed gets killed outright!'

Muhammed smiled. A pretty young WAC nurse in khaki was approaching them, the single gold bar of a second lieutenant on her shoulder. He had eyes only for her. With elaborate courtesy he saluted her, then winked knowingly. Her shy smile changed to a blush. She pushed past them hurriedly.

'Give over, Muhammed,' Peters said. 'You're embarrassing the lady.'

'That reminds me,' Stevens remarked dourly, 'I ain't had the Christmas present Commander Mallory promised me yet.'

They passed through the hospital's gloomy reception hall, its only concession to the festive spirit a mean Christmas tree on which the candles flickered weakly every time the big swing door opened to admit the stretcher-bearers with their grim burdens. They put on their caps and went out onto the street.

It looked like snow again. The December sky was leaden and overcast. On their side of the street a line of boxlike camouflaged ambulances was moving up to the entrance, each one bearing a sign and its windscreen stating that it was 'Carrying Casualties.'

'Poor buggers,' Stevens said, as they hurried over to where Crooke and Commander Mallory were waiting for them in a borrowed US staff car.

'How's he getting on?' Crooke asked anxiously.

'All right, sir,' Peters answered. 'The Yankee M.O. says he's on the mend. He's a tough old bird, the Yank is.'

'I'm glad to hear that Jones is all right,' Commander Mallory said, reaching for a cigarette. 'As soon as the weather clears, I'm going to get the Moonlight Squadron to send over a Lysander to pick him up and fly him to the UK for special treatment.'

'We are getting fancy now, aren't we?' Stevens sniffed. 'VIP treatment is it now! The Destroyers are coming up in the world. But talking about VIP treatment, sir, I've got a little bone to pick with you.'

'Save the nibbling till later,' Mallory said. 'We've got other things to do first.'

They drove in silence for a few minutes until Mallory pulled up outside the SIS's Paris headquarters.

Philby was waiting for them in the gloomy hall. At the little reception desk behind him the pudgy Intelligence Corps sergeant was passed out drunk, an empty glass clutched in his pale hand.

Philby caught Crooke's disgusted look. 'The spirit of Christmas p-p-past,' he said. 'Stewed as a b-b-bloody newt!' He led them into the inner office. 'A belated Merry Christmas to you a-a-all and the warmest of greetings f-f-from "C".' He waved them to a seat. 'Take a pew.'

'And what has "C" to report?' Mallory asked coldly, in his best Old Etonian manner. Philby had obviously been celebrating the festive season himself.

'Good news. What was l-l-left in the bottle can be analysed after all. Soon we'll know whether the boffins can get rid of us j-j-just like that.' He snapped his fingers together and laughed. 'Me, I'll s-s-stick to that.' He indicated the half empty bottle of calvados on the table. 'Like gin in Manchester on a w-w-wet Wednesday, it's the best way of getting out of Paris on a s-s-snowy Sunday.'

'So I see,' Crooke said; his distaste for the SIS agent was obvious. 'But before you leave us with the aid of your calvados, Mr Philby, what about the chap who organized the raid on the villa — that Sergeant White?'

Philby grinned. Deliberately he took a deep swig and wiped his mouth with the back of his hand. 'Hm, that was g-g-good! Oh, our people traced him as far as P-P-Portbou on the Spanish frontier. Then the c-c-clods lost him. But I have no doubt that he will t-t-turn up one of these days.'

He took another drink of calvados.

'You may be p-p-pleased to know that "C" has a-a-approved your belated Christmas p-p-present from Eisenhower. The War Office will allow you to accept the Legion of M-M-Merit he wants to give you for this operation.'

'Thank you,' the Commander said coldly.

Philby looked at the Destroyers. 'He's also fixed it up with the Army's legal branch that y-y-you don't have to go inside again, although apparently y-y-you severely injured some sergeant-major or other. He walks with a l-l-limp now.'

'Black Jack,' Stevens snorted. 'I hope the bastard gets sodding piles from it too.'

'But "C" turned down the Bronze Star for y-y-you.' Philby sat down suddenly and almost upset what was left of the bottle of calvados.

'What's this, Mallory?' Crooke asked.

'Well, Eisenhower has awarded Stead the Silver Star and recommended you lot should be given the Bronze Star. I forwarded the recommendation to London for approval. But, as you have heard, the powers-that-be have turned it down.'

Crooke laughed cynically. 'I wonder what the Destroyers will have to do before the military establishment is convinced we are not just a bunch of worthless rogues, good enough for missions like this — and that's about all?'

'Simple, sir,' Stevens cut in smartly. 'Get our bloody heads blown off! Then the Destroyers'll be respectable at last — the day they're pushing up daisies in Brown's Garden.' He turned to Mallory. 'But before that day comes along, sir, I'd like to pick my bone with you.'

'Fire away then, Stevens.'

'You remember sir that you promised me something when this op was over?'

'Did I?'

'Yes, sir, you promised me the biggest, most expensive bit o' crackling in Paris.' He puffed his chest out. 'Okay, Commander, after that last little lot, I'm good and ready for her. I want me Christmas Box *now*.'

For a moment Commander Mallory seemed too astonished to reply. Then abruptly his well-bred reserve vanished. 'Dammit, Stevens,' he cried, 'you're right! And you shall have her!' He turned to the other Destroyers, ignoring Philby altogether. 'Come on — the lot of you! They say you can do Paris only once in a lifetime — let's do it now!'

'M-m-my God!' Philby stuttered. 'The m-m-millennium has arrived! The rich are fraternizing with the masses!' He giggled and passed out.

A NOTE TO THE READER

Dear Reader,

If you have enjoyed this novel enough to leave a review on **Amazon** and **Goodreads**, then we would be truly grateful.

Sapere Books

Sapere Books is an exciting new publisher of brilliant fiction and popular history.

To find out more about our latest releases and our monthly bargain books visit our website: **saperebooks.com**

www.ingramcontent.com/pod-product-compliance
Lightning Source LLC
Chambersburg PA
CBHW060349180626
46817CB00008B/2955